QUILTED LANDSCAPE

Conversations with Young Immigrants

YALE STROM

Simon & Schuster Books for Young Readers

Acknowledgments

I would like to thank the following people and institutions who helped to make this book possible: Dr. Leonard Golubchik, Faye Oldak, Marta Stewart, Willie Mac and David Datta of P.S. 20 (Anna Silver School) and Ronnie Loeschelle of New York City; Laurie Greenbaum and Maraya Avrasin of Sarasota; Sharon Milch of River Dell High School of Oradell, N.J.; Clifford Cohen, Genevieve Lovitt, and Daremyelesh Yegazu of Los Angeles; Carmen Valenzuela, Manuel H. Paul, Rita Byers, Brian Blue and Mary Kay Blue of Byer Middle School, San Ysidro, CA; Ernie McCray and Alembunch Fesseha of John G. Marvin Elementary and Phyllis and David Strom of San Diego, CA; Marilyn Heckmyer of McCracken Middle School, Skokie, IL; Ira and Beth Fenton of Northbrook, IL; Sue Bernstein of Chicago; Heather Mitchell of ACCESS, Dearborn, MI; Cynthia Wilson and Dan L. Rickerd of Parkway Heights Middle School, South San Francisco; Andy and Melinda Jones of San Bruno, CA; Kitty Prager of St. John's Preparatory School, Astoria, NY; Naomi Shihab Nye of San Antonio, TX; and Steven Posen, Mika Yoshida, David G. Imber, Linda Kalnina of the Latvian Mission to the United Nations and HIAS of New York City. All of the above provided me with invaluable help and/or hospitality. Special thanks to J's Lab in Oak Park, Michigan, for its careful and timely work in printing the photographs. I express extreme gratitude to my agent, Mary Jack Wald, who brought my idea for this book to Stephanie Owens Lurie, who believed in this project from the beginning. My added thanks to Andrea Schneeman, and my wife, Elizabeth. Most of all, I thank my editor and friend, Virginia Duncan, whose insight, enthusiasm and tenacity were essential to my completing this project.

 SIMON & SCHUSTER BOOKS FOR YOUNG READERS

An imprint of Simon & Schuster Children's Publishing Division

1230 Avenue of the Americas, New York, New York 10020

Copyright © 1996 by Yale Strom

All rights reserved including the right of reproduction in whole or in part in any form.

SIMON & SCHUSTER BOOKS FOR YOUNG READERS is a trademark of Simon & Schuster.

Book design by Virginia Pope

Maps by Robert Romagnoli

The text for this book is set in ITC Garamond

Printed and bound in the United States of America

First Edition

10 9 8 7 6 5 4 3 2 1

Library of Congress Cataloging-in-Publication Data

Strom, Yale. Quilted landscape / Yale Strom. — 1st ed.

         p.   cm.   Includes index.

Summary: Twenty-six young people of different ages and nationalities describe their experience of leaving their countries and immigrating to the United States.

ISBN 0-689-80074-6

1. Children of immigrants—United States—Biography—Juvenile literature. 2. United States—Emigration and immigration—Juvenile literature. [1. Immigrants—United States. 2. United States—Emigration and immigration.] I. Title.

E184.A1S896 1996

305.8'00973—dc20 95-45150

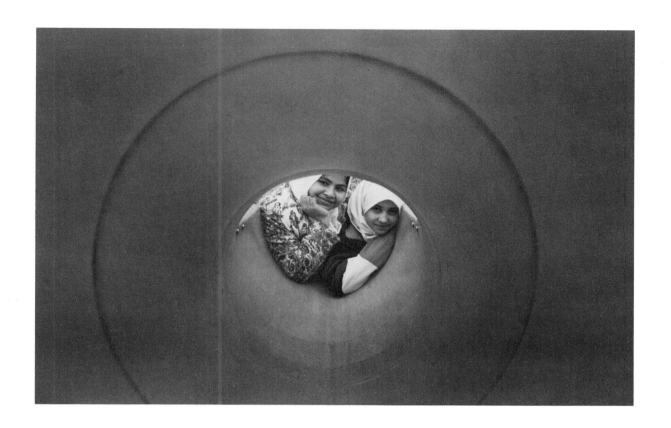

"By nature all men are alike;
it was by custom and habit that they are set apart."

"In education there is no distinction of classes."

- Confucius

Contents

Introduction

The word "immigrant" comes from the Latin *immigrareatus*, which means "to move in." People have been moving to the North American continent since well before recorded history—nomadic tribes from the steppes of Asia, Scandinavian Vikings, slaves from Africa, farmers from Europe, explorers and laborers and intellectuals from all over the globe. Some were fascinated by the unknown; some came seeking land, wealth, jobs, or freedom from persecution. Others were given no choice, and were brought over as slaves. All of these peoples and their descendants have created a nation of immigrants—a quilt of languages, traditions, cultures, histories and heritages. Now, at the turn of the millennium, new faces are still arriving. In the 1990s, nearly one million immigrants enter this country legally and illegally each year.

In the 1950s, Europeans accounted for two-thirds of all newcomers to the U.S. In the 1980s, their share dropped to 15%. The largest group of immigrants in recent years is from Asia (36%), and a close 34% of new residents are from North and Central America—a number which is steadily increasing. In 1990, the number of immigrants arriving from Latin America and the Caribbean surpassed the number coming from Europe for the first time in U.S. history.

Young people make up over one-third of the immigrant population of the United States. They come primarily from Mexico (21%), the Dominican Republic (8%), the former Soviet Union (7%), the Philippines (6%), and Vietnam (4%). Though these young people and their families can be found in even the smallest towns across the nation, they move in the greatest numbers to metropolitan areas in California (26%), New York (18%), Florida (7%), Texas (7%), New Jersey (5%), and Illinois (5%).*

I targeted many of these areas when interviewing young people for this book, and I relied primarily on my own contacts and those of my friends to locate the subjects of the interviews. Often I was first introduced to them at their schools by a trusted teacher or principal, and then we moved to the library or a quiet section of the playground where other children would not interrupt us as we talked. Sometimes an interpreter or a friend would accompany us if I was unable to speak the interviewee's native language, or, in the case of girls, if they could not be left alone with a man for cultural or religious reasons.

Often, when the interviewees returned to class after our conversation and told their classmates they were going to be in a book, a sudden swarm of volunteers presented itself. One day a child yelled proudly, "I told you I was going to be famous one day…it just happened a lot sooner than I had planned!"

Though energetic, eager to learn English, and anxious to be accepted by their native-born peers, most of these young people have experienced the same problems that have confronted new residents since the great wave of immigration to the United States during the years 1881 to 1924. With anti-immigration sentiment on the rise, some have to cope with hostility of individuals, of a community, or of government legislation (such as California's "Proposition 187," a measure which denies social services and public education to illegal immigrants) but healthy optimism and pride in their cultural heritage helps to keep them strong.

Many of these students also begin to encounter generational conflicts between themselves and their parents and grandparents. They must find their own identity, separate from (but not exclusive of) the culture in which their parents came of age. In addition, parents who had limited or no formal schooling in their native country sometimes believe that obtaining a job skill and providing additional income for the family is of greater importance than education. Their children may have to work for pay or do the shopping, laundry, and banking because the parents speak little or no English. Suddenly, the adults have become dependents, and this role reversal can have a damaging effect on the fragile structure of a family in transition.

But for all the problems these immigrant youth face, their parents face even larger difficulties: finding full-time work and housing while learning a new language and maintaining self-esteem. As Christian Tico, a young immigrant from Romania noted, "As youth we are like fresh, pliable clay, but as you become older, like my parents, the clay loses its flexibility and eventually hardens."

Every year, curiosity and personal pride in cultural heritage brings over two million tourists to the Statue of Liberty and Ellis Island in New York City. Inscribed on the Statue of Liberty is Emma Lazarus' eloquent welcome to immigrants from the renowned poem "The New Colossus":

> Give me your tired, your poor,
> your huddled masses yearning to breathe free …
> Send these, the homeless, tempest-tost to me.
> I lift my lamp beside the golden door!

As the millennium approaches, the pride that native-born residents once took in these sentiments is in danger of fading. Intolerance and controversy often surround discussions of immigration and its future role in our society. I have always cherished those many faces, foods, fashions, languages, religions, and traditions that run through the fabric of this country. As I traveled across the United States, I saw how this diverse nation represents the land of promise and opportunity for those outside its borders. These interviews helped me to remember that our shared visions—as different as they may be—hold the same echoes of hope, humor, perseverance, and pride.

—*Yale Strom*

Arctic Ocean

ASIA

EUROPE

Riga, Latvia
Borisov, Belarus
Mukachevo, Ukraine
Bucharest, Romania

Tbilisi, Georgia

Chittagong,
Bangladesh

Hilapur,
Bangladesh

Tokyo, Japan

Antalya,
Turkey

Iran

Pacific

Greece

Iraklion,
Crete

Egypt

Beirut,
Lebanon

Fuzhou,
China

Famar and Zambales, Philippines

Manilla, Philippines

AFRICA

Al-Farwānīyah,
Kuwait

San'a,
Yemen

Bangkok,
Thailand

Bulalacao, Philippines

Ocean

Teklahaimanot,
Ethiopia

Piliyandala,
Sri Lanka

Indian

Djakarta, Indonesia

Suva, Fiji

Ocean

AUSTRALIA

RR

Christian Tico

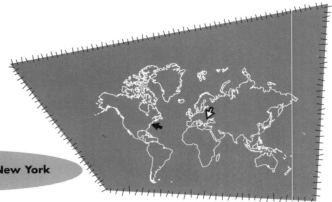

Age 17

Born in Bucharest, Romania

Lives in Queens, New York

Christian Tico

> I know it's going to be harder, but what's life without a challenge.

My father's grandmother was Greek and his father was Albanian and I'm Romanian. But I should say I'm Romanian-American. My father and his family moved to Romania after World War II.

Romania is a beautiful country but after the Ceaușescu years it was difficult. We had a big house but food was scarce. I didn't worry about the freedoms we didn't have. Most things seemed all right. You know when you are young you usually worry about personal comforts, never politics. I'd like to go back to Bucharest but I'm not sure when this will be.

After we left Romania we went to Italy and stayed with my mother's sister for six months. In Romania everything that has to do with bureaucracy takes a long time. It took several years to get our papers in order. While living in Italy I almost spoke fluent Italian. Then when we moved into this neighborhood in Queens, everybody was Italian and they all spoke Italian to me. They thought I was Italian. I have forgotten much of my Italian, but not Romanian.

We try to keep some Romanian customs like going to the Greek Orthodox church where they have a mass in the Romanian liturgy. I go to the Catholic mass here at St. John's but outside of school never. I speak Romanian at home but it's hard to find others to speak with outside my home.

Next year instead of going to twelfth grade I'll be going to St. John's University. I'm in this program that lets me take advanced classes my junior year so I'm able to go into college my senior year. I'm excited about it. After school I play sports, do some reading, play a little guitar, I'm pretty bad actually, and I write. I love writing, especially poetry.

I think if an immigrant family leaves a country that is politically undesirable and their kids are young, the kids will adjust pretty easily. For an adult it's something totally different. You come as an adult, you don't know the language and you are trying so hard to support a family. There is a lot of—a tremendous amount of—stress parents go through trying to adjust and fit into American culture, and at the same time earn a living. After six months of being here my father was dead. The stress killed him. He died of a heart attack. Kids don't realize how hard it is for their parents to start a new life in a new country.

My father was an archaeologist in Romania but lost his job when they knew he was going to leave Romania. During those years they often took reprisals—they being the government—against those who wanted to leave.

When they first came here my parents had to work in jobs that they wouldn't normally have done in Romania. My mother worked in a factory, my father as a waiter. Could you imagine having your master's in a science and being forced to make a living by being a waiter? This bothered my father—I know it—but he tried never to show that side of him.

My mom wants to go back to school and get her nursing degree. She is fifty-three but wants to pursue her dream. She has a nursing degree from Romania, but she can't transfer her credits here. They won't accept them. She has the knowledge.

When I hear old people and young people speaking badly about immigrants it just doesn't make sense to me. We were all immigrants one time. In California it is crazy to take away the education from these illegal immigrants. When they become adults they will still be there, many of them, but not productive.

Romanian people happen to be rather racist. They often speak poorly about people of color. I can't believe some of the things my mom says. Being brought up in a neighborhood and a school like St. John's prepares you for the real world of diverse peoples and cultures. In Romania the Gypsies are mistreated mainly because they are darker and have a different cultural

The Immigrant's Journey

The immigrant's journey is
not unlike that of the hero's . . .
And I feign not from calling him a hero,
Because that's just what my father was.

To leave one's home is
a nomadic act . . .
And immigrants are modern nomads,
They are restless like my mother is.

The immigrant's journey is
unconscious and internalized . . .
And the goal is within, not without,
It is the hope of what I will be.

Christian Tico

Christian wrote this poem in memory of his father.

ROMANIA

SIZE: 237,499 square kilometers (91,699 square miles), somewhat smaller than New York and Pennsylvania combined

POPULATION: 23,505,000

CAPITAL: Bucharest (population 2,450,984)

ETHNICITIES: Romanian, Magyar, Rom (Gypsy), German, Ukrainian, Serb, Croat, Turk, Russian, Jewish, Greek, Armenian

RELIGIONS: Romanian Orthodox, Roman Catholic, Calvinist, Lutheran, Baptist, Pentecostal, Jewish, Russian Orthodox, Greek Orthodox

LANGUAGES: Romanian, Hungarian

MONETARY UNIT: leu

BECAME INDEPENDENT: December 30, 1881

INTERNATIONALLY KNOWN ROMANIANS: Nadia Comaneci (Olympic gymnast), George Enescu (composer), Eugene Ionescu (playwright)

TRADITIONAL FOODS: mamaliga (polenta)

✽ The character of Dracula was based on a real-life Romanian hero of the middle ages, Prince Vlad (Dracul) Tepeş, "The Impaler." He helped defeat the Turks who invaded the province of Wallacha in the fourteenth century.

Christian takes the subway home from school.

history. I think in general too many people spend their energies on looking at what the differences are between us instead of at what the similarities are. My mom is not a bad person, she just was brought up in a country that is rather chauvinistic when it comes to accepting others who are different from yourself.

Sport is the great equalizer. When I'm playing soccer we have to play and communicate as a team. We are black, Spanish, Greek, Irish, Romanian, Polish, and Indian on the team. I don't care what anyone eats in their home, what church they go to, or what their skin color is, if he can't dribble the soccer ball or defend his goal he's no help to us.

Marion Boteju

Age 16

Born in Leicester, England

Lives in Queens, New York

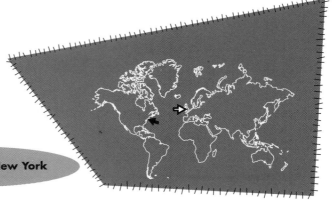

Marion Boteju

My parents were set on giving us a better education and they really believed in the motto "America, the land of opportunity," so we moved here.

We came to America by way of Sri Lanka. I lived in a very nice residential area outside the main center of town called Piliyandala. It was an area with lots of farms, few buildings and mountains. When I walked to school in the mornings I passed rice paddies and beautiful trees. It's not like here—wall-to-wall buildings.

School was definitely much more strict. I went to an all-girls school. School was easy there but it is far easier here. We spoke English often in the home so I didn't have a language problem. Actually it was more difficult to learn Sinhala.

When I wasn't in school on the weekends, on Sundays we went to church. The days felt longer there. Even though I had a longer school day, from 7:30 A.M. to 3:30 P.M., we had a lot of time to play.

I want to be a defense attorney. It must be incredible to be in the heat of the moment when every word you can say can save someone. I find that a great challenge.

Marion walks around her neighborhood in Astoria, New York.

My cousins would come over and play cricket or just talk and take walks in the fields.

The days just seemed longer there. I think this was because the pace of our lives was slower, more relaxed than here. My perception then was that I was able to do more in a day than here.

I miss my cousins, my home, the mountains. I'll always call Sri Lanka my home. But even though I miss my home there are certain opportunities here in America that one can't get in Sri Lanka. I'll visit often, or as often as I have the time and money. I might move to England after college.

The music I listen to is mostly from the eighties like REO Speedwagon, Air Supply, and Chicago. I don't like rap, but reggae is fun to dance to.

My mom was here first. Then my brothers and I came. Afterward my dad came. We came in the summer so I had time to adjust. When I first walked into my sixth grade class everyone turned around and looked at me. I felt a bit uncomfortable but after three days I had several friends. Getting used to the country wasn't difficult. There were teenagers who bothered my brother and me once when we were walking in the neighborhood. They

SIZE: 65,610 square kilometers (25,332 square miles), about the size of West Virginia

POPULATION: 18,346,000

CAPITAL: Colombo (population 1,262,000)

ETHNICITIES: Sinhalese, Tamils, Muslims, Baluchis, Veddahs, Burghers, Malays, Sri Lankan aborigines, Kuravans

RELIGIONS: Buddhism, Hinduism, Islam, Christianity

LANGUAGES: Sinhala, Tamil, English

MONETARY UNIT: Sri Lankan rupee

BECAME INDEPENDENT: February 4, 1948

TRADITIONAL FOODS: paan (bread), dello (cuttle fish dish), kukulmas (spicy chicken dish)

INTERNATIONALLY KNOWN SRI LANKANS: Sirimavo Bandaranaike (the world's first woman prime minister, 1960), Nanda Malani (classical, folk singer)

✽ Arab traders knew the island as "Serendip," root of *serendipity*. Sri Lanka changed its name from Ceylon in 1972. Some of the finest teas in the world originate from this region.

thought we were Indians and called us names. This was the first time it had happened to me so I didn't even know how to react or feel. It hasn't happened again.

If you say anyone actually belongs in America that would be the Native Americans, because everyone else originated from England and other countries. No one has the right to say this is my country, you can't live here. I suppose this is just human nature—being defensive when you see others coming to your territory. These people who say this, like these right wing militia organizations, have the right to think these thoughts but as soon as they try to inhibit me in any way from living where I want to in America, then there is a problem.

Even though I wasn't born in Sri Lanka the culture is important to me. I will want my children to know who they are, where they come from, know the language and be proud of their heritage. My mom cooks Sri Lankan food which is very spicy. We eat rice every day just like others who eat bread every day. We are taught to honor and respect our elders. If you are the youngest you have to listen to your brothers. My brothers don't force anything on me, but I have to show complete respect for them.

Personally if I meet someone who is not Sri Lankan and I love him I would marry that person. Naturally if you find someone from your own culture then you already share many things between you. But without respect and love for your spouse it doesn't matter if you are from the same culture, religion, or race, your marriage will fail.

I love going to school with a lot of different people. In my country it was just Sinhalese and Tamils. I've gotten to learn a lot about other cultures, their family life, just the way they look at things. This school experience helps prepare you for the big world out there.

Chao Jing Weng

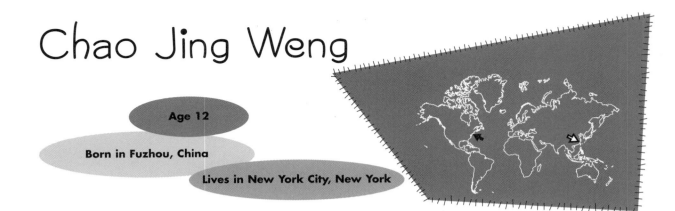

Age 12

Born in Fuzhou, China

Lives in New York City, New York

I was born in Fuzhou where I began school when I was seven. School there was the same as here except in China you went home and ate lunch. We began school at 7:20 A.M. and came home at 10:45 A.M. and then returned to school at 1:30 P.M. In school I learned to read Chinese but not to write. I speak good Chinese and always will because we speak only this language in my home.

Chao Jing works on the computer in school.

I'm not sure why we came to America. My father was here about eight or nine years before us. My father works in New Jersey as a busboy. My mother is not working. She stays at home. I have one brother and two sisters.

I like United States because I can do whatever I want to here. But I don't think there is a big difference between United States and China except that in China we all look the same—same eyes, hair and skin color.

After school in Fuzhou, I would do my homework and then play running games with my cousin. I liked my house better in China because we don't live in a house in the United States. Our house was bigger, with a rectangular roof. I don't like living in an apartment because each month I have to give them $660. I mean my father pays the money. In China my father owned the house. A busboy doesn't make a lot of money so $660 every month isn't easy to pay.

> The most difficult thing for me when I came here was not coming here but leaving China.

When I get older I want to help my parents. Maybe I can get a job with computers and give them some of my money. In China we say it is the job for children to take care of their parents when they become older. Do American-born children feel the same way?

I don't listen to music or paint because that bores me. I just love to do computers in my free time. Sometimes I read books my sister brings home from the library.

You know it is not easy for a young Chinese boy to leave his home and come to a country where the language and customs are different. I have many uncles and cousins in China. Maybe if I would have been an adult I wouldn't have moved here with my mother.

Sometimes a few kids in this school call me "Chino." I don't know why they call me this. It makes me very sad. But I still like going to a school with many different people. In China I went to school only with

> We had television in Fuzhou, but only my last three years before I left. My favorite television program here is <u>Power Rangers</u>.

Chinese. I never saw an American in Fuzhou. When Americans travel to China they go to Hong Kong or places close by. Once when I was in second grade a white came to my city. I didn't see him but all of my friends told me. Because I went to school earlier in the day I missed him. He came to the school in the afternoon.

My father speaks a little English, but my mother nothing. When we go to the store, bank, or post office, I help them by speaking English. At the bank it is usually my sister who helps because I am too small.

We have only two rooms in our apartment. I sleep with my brother and two sisters in one room and my father and mother sleep in the other room. It is quite crowded for $660 a month. Does this mean an apartment with four rooms would cost $1,320 a month? We had more room in Fuzhou, but coming to a new country probably isn't easy for anyone.

CHINA

OFFICIAL NAME: People's Republic of China
SIZE: 9,600,000 square kilometers (3,691,000 miles)
POPULATION: 1,238,319,000
CAPITAL: Beijing (population 7,362,425)
ETHNICITIES: Han, Chinese, Zhuang, Manchu, Mongol, Buyi, Korean, Hui, Uygurs, Yi, Miao, Tibetans, Yao, Bai, Hani
RELIGIONS: Confucianism, Taoism, Buddhism, Islam, Christianity (China is officially atheist)
LANGUAGES: standard Chinese (Putonghua), and many local dialects
MONETARY UNIT: yuan
BECAME INDEPENDENT: Under the Qin Dynasty, in 221 B.C.; then the Qing (Manchu) Dynasty was replaced by the Republic on February 12, 1912. The People's Republic was established October 1, 1949.
TRADITIONAL FOODS: nan-ru (fermented red bean curd), lo-bo (Chinese radish)
INTERNATIONALLY KNOWN CHINESE: Mao Zedung (founder of the People's Republic), Joan Chen (actress), Wayne Wang (film director)
✳ China is the oldest continuous major world civilization, with records dating back 3,500 years. It is also the most populous country in the world.

Yan Fang Zheng

Age 12

Born in Fuzhou, China

Lives in New York City, New York

I was born in China, in Fuzhou. I came to America in 1993 with my mother, brother, and three sisters. I don't know why we came here, we just came. In my house in New York City I live with my cousins and sister. My mother lives in the Bronx.

When I was born I got very sick, very sick. My mother thought I was going to die so she gave me to some other people. And this other person didn't have a daughter, just two sons. And these people are very nice. The father is my father's best friend.

Yan Fang Zheng

My school in Fuzhou is very poor because the building is very old and broken. We learned many things at this school, math, science, Chinese, and art. In art I like drawing the best. When I was young I was always drawing. This is what I did when I was playing.

Before I came here it was difficult to leave. My real mother had to go to another city and convince the police officers I was her daughter. At first they didn't believe her so I wasn't allowed to come here. After much money, which my mother gave to the police officers, I was allowed to leave.

> When I watch TV I like to watch cartoons and movies about ghosts. I like being scared. I never go to the movies with my sisters because we don't have money.

I was sad when I left because my other mother stayed behind. I have two mothers, one living in the Bronx and one living in Fuzhou. I love both my mothers the same and both my fathers the same. I am also writing letters to my brothers in Fuzhou, to my Fuzhou mother's sons.

Yan Fang paints in her art class.

I will always remember Chinese and not forget how to read, write and speak the language. We speak only Chinese in my home. The hardest thing about coming to New York was learning English.

In Mrs. Oldak's class I have new friends who are from other countries besides China. In my school in Fuzhou you never saw a student with red hair and blue eyes, always black hair and brown eyes. Sometimes it can be boring seeing children who look the same as the students in my school that was in Fuzhou.

In Fuzhou we didn't have computers. I learned about computers here in this country.

I want to become a lawyer when I'm older because a lawyer knows everything. I wanted to do maybe drawing, but my mother in the Bronx doesn't want me to. She and my sisters said I won't be able to succeed when I grow up if I do drawing.

My home in Fuzhou was better than my home here. Here my home is so dark, it has only two small windows. In Fuzhou we lived near many mountains and beautiful beaches. I did go to the beach here at Coney Island. It was fun. But the streets around my home here are much dirtier. Sometimes I clean the sidewalk near my house.

After school I walk home, do my homework, wash my clothes by hand, then eat dinner, usually Chinese food—rice, vegetables, and fish—but never meat. I hate meat.

Every weekend I go to visit my mother and father in the Bronx. They work there too in a Chinese restaurant. I go by myself every Friday afternoon by subway to the Bronx. I'm never scared.

When I get married I will only be with a Chinese man because my mother hates the white man. She only likes the Chinese man, not even Japanese or Korean.

I don't believe in God because my mother in the Bronx doesn't believe. My mother in China, she believes. We don't celebrate Christmas, we celebrate the Chinese New Year. This year is the year of the pig. I celebrated with my mom. We got some new clothes and some money. Normally the parents give

Yan Fang made a drawing of her neighborhood in Fuzhou.

their children one hundred or five hundred dollars, but my mother just gave me fifty dollars. We don't have so much money, but I am happy. This fifty dollars I just saved. I save it in a little jar in my house. I want to buy some books and pens. If my pens are broken then I can buy some new pens for drawing.

I don't like the people who hit and don't like the Chinese. I think they do this because Chinese are short and they are tall. I also don't like American food like pizza and McDonald's hamburgers. The taste of these foods doesn't seem fresh.

In Fuzhou I listened to the old ones, to the old Chinese music. Here my mother listens to the old ones too. Here I like to listen to the black man sing and watch how they dance, it is really good. I had never seen a black man in China. When I first saw him here I was scared because he was so tall. But this man is friendly and I'm not scared.

Carlos Nuñez

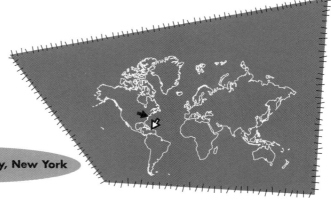

Age 10

Born in Santo Domingo, Dominican Republic

Lives in New York City, New York

Carlos Nuñez

I was excited about coming here because I wanted to play in the snow, make snowmen and have snowball fights.

I liked school in Santo Domingo because I had a lot of friends. We would play lots of different games. My favorites were Monopoly, basketball and baseball.

I came to America in 1993. My grandfather came to Dominican to get my mother, aunt, cousin, and myself. This was the first time I had ever been on an airplane.

Over there you only hear Spanish being spoken, never English. Here in my neighborhood you hear Spanish and English. We lived in a house, which I like better than the apartment we have here. There I played with my cousins downstairs outside. Here my mother won't let me play outside. I have to play in the house. She thinks something's going to happen to me. There is trouble sometimes, even killings happening in our neighborhood. My mother is afraid that I could be hurt.

I'll never forget how to speak Spanish. If I forget I won't be able to speak to my mother. Then I won't be able to tell what I want her to buy and where and when I want to go somewhere.

Coming here wasn't difficult for me because I like traveling to new places. What I think about most is I will never be able to save enough money to be able to visit my homeland, my friends and cousins.

My mother read something to me from the newspaper about people in America who don't like new immigrants. This makes me sad. These people come here to get a better life, to get a better education. My mother came here to get a better life. And these people who speak badly about new immigrants forget that their people once came from another country too. Maybe many years ago these people should not have been allowed to come and stay here.

I live with my mother, sister, cousin, my other cousin, my aunt and my other aunt and my grandpa all in two rooms. I sleep in a bed with my mother and sister. My two aunts and two cousins sleep in another bed and my grandpa, he sleeps in the hallway on a sofa between the bedroom and the toilet.

We have to stay here for now because my mother doesn't have enough money to get another house. She is working to get another house.

My father lives in Dominican. I don't know if he will move here or not. My mother takes me to this store where you can call people who live far away and I speak with my father. I miss him because he would take me places, like the beach and park and we would play baseball. My sister or mother don't play baseball with me.

I play trombone and French horn after school in Mr. Mac's class. We play the song "Rose con Leche." I don't practice at home because my mother doesn't want to hear me blowing in such a small house, and she says the instrument could get lost. When I am older I will become a music teacher like Mr. Mac. I like playing and teaching other kids how to play music. At home I listen to Spanish, reggae, and rap music, but Spanish is my favorite kind.

Carlos fools around in his classroom during recess.

SIZE: 48,442 square kilometers (18,704 square miles), about the size of Vermont

POPULATION: 7.3 million

CAPITAL: Santo Domingo (population 2.5 million)

ETHNICITIES: Caucasian, African origin, mixed

RELIGION: Christianity (Roman Catholic)

LANGUAGE: Spanish

MONETARY UNIT: peso oro

BECAME INDEPENDENT: February 27, 1844

TRADITIONAL FOODS: plantains, rice, beans

INTERNATIONALLY KNOWN DOMINICANS: Juan Marichal (Hall of Fame baseball player), Gaston Fernando Delinge (poet), Juan Bosch (writer and former President)

✱ The island of Hispaniola, of which the Dominican Republic forms the eastern two-thirds, and Haiti the remainder, was originally occupied by members of the Taino tribe. The sweet potato originates from the Taino. They called it *batata* which means sweet potato in many languages throughout the world.

Carlos in class

I like going to a school like PS 20 that has students from different countries. I learn about their customs, food, and games. In this school I have met students from Bangladesh, Japan, China, Mexico, and Peru. But I guess if you think about it one day New York could fill up with too many people. It seems everyone from other countries wants to come here and live. When it becomes too crowded here then those moving here might go instead to Nebraska or Montana. I'm sure the streets are cleaner there than they are in New York City.

Khandakar Mita

Age 11

Born in Hilapur, Bangladesh

Lives in New York City, New York

Khandakar Mita in the doorway of her home in Manhattan.

I was born in Bangladesh in the district of Noakhali in a village called Hilapur, but I was raised in Chittagong. My country is a very beautiful country. I like my country. We have many different kinds of wildflowers and birds. Here in New York City you have to go to a flower shop to see such beautiful flowers. In my hometown I just went outside of my home.

My father was living and working here in America and we missed him very much so we joined him. I came here for the education. My desire is to grow to my full potential in America. I like this country as much as Bangladesh.

When I think about Bangladesh I become sad because my mother is still there. I miss her greatly. I have two brothers and no sisters. One brother is sixteen years and the other is nine years. My mother is alone in Bangladesh taking care of our two homes. She will be joining us soon.

I didn't have any problems adjusting to this country. It was just as I thought. Before I came here it was my intense desire to come, that's why I didn't have any problems adjusting. There was nothing I didn't like here. Nobody here has bothered me, called me names, or started a fight. All the kids are nice. However, I have heard some kids and their parents say some things about too many immigrants coming to America. America is too crowded and they are taking our jobs away. When I hear this it makes me

> Whatever I'll take from this country I will give back by working here and being a kind person in society.

feel very sad. If they would come to my country they wouldn't hear such words. I would never say these things because it would hurt their feelings. What jobs are we taking away anyway? Cleaning restaurants, waiting on tables, cleaning apartments or working in magazine kiosks.

I am Muslim and I believe it is good to pray to Allah. We believe if you don't do your *namaj* [prayers] it will be harmful for you. If I ask Allah anything he will provide it for me. Though I'm Bengali and Muslim it doesn't mean I have to marry a Bengali. I judge people by their qualities. I like a person who is nice and honest in all ways. It doesn't matter what religion the person is.

Because I am Muslim I am participating in Ramadan. We fast all day, eating and drinking nothing until sunset so we know a little of the pain millions of starving poor people are feeling around the world. Rich people who have never gone to bed hungry know nothing about poverty.

When I grow up I want to be an engineer. A good engineer building different things. When I become a good engineer I will work in this country, not in Bangladesh, because this country helped me to get a good education. I want to give my knowledge and skills back to this government.

In Bangladesh, society usually favors the boys, but my father didn't look at me in that traditional way. He believes in equality between girls and boys. Whatever a boy can do a girl can do just as well. My father always tells my mother that my daughter and sons are equal.

The women in America dress differently than we do in Bangladesh. In my country we wear saris, *salwar* [long dresses] and *karneez* [tops], which cover our bodies—not like hot pants.

Khandakar stands next to Mr. Mac, her music teacher, in the schoolyard.

Manolis Pahakis

Age 17

Born in Iráklion, Crete

Lives in Queens, New York

I'm from Greece, the Greek island Crete. My city, Iráklion, comes from the name of the mythic semigod, semiman Herakles. He was supposed to have been there.

I came to Astoria in September 1994. I came mainly because of the better educational system; we have a lot of troubles in Greece with education. Every school is public and supported by the government. The Greek economy has been struggling so the schools have been suffering. We don't have as many educa-

> ## When I first came here I found it strange that everyone seems to be talking about money.

tional materials or such nice buildings, but the level of education they offer us was much higher than here. It's like the whole student body there gets the level of education that the honor students get here. Of course not every student there takes advantage of this. However, the problem that made me decide to come here was that only 30 percent of the high school graduates get into college. You have to take these very difficult exams to get accepted into college and I was reluctant about this.

First I came with my mother. She stayed for three months. Then she went back to Greece and she will return here to see me graduate this year. I live here by myself in an apartment. I miss my brother the most. He had difficulties with his college entrance exams and is now going into the army.

I also miss my island, the people, the sun, everything. I intend to go back to Crete after I finish college here. But maybe I'll stay here if the job opportunities are better. I'm not sure yet what profession I'll study. I'm interested in poetry, biology—we will see what will happen.

One thing I found here is people don't touch each other as much. We touch, hug, kiss, hold hands, but in America if men do this we are looked at as if we are a bit strange, abnormal, perhaps homosexual. The Mediterranean way is much warmer.

The simplicity in America sometimes reaches the level of ignorance. I think many Americans' historical view of the world is seen through a shallow vision. I'm not saying simplicity is bad. In fact many Europeans do not achieve simplicity because they think their culture is so much higher than everybody else's. By simplicity I mean living life like a single thread that is woven in a shirt. That thread is one of many and can be lost in the entire mass of threads. By itself it has a certain beauty, but needs the strength of the other threads to become something whole and strong.

The hardest thing to get used to here was the schedule. We sleep more in Crete. My normal day back home was, wake up at 8 A.M., be in school at 8:30 A.M., be home at 2:30 P.M. and eat dinner. Then we would take a nap and get up and take private tutor lessons from 7 P.M. to 10 P.M. Then we would come home, study a little more, or just immediately go to sleep. Sometimes we would go out even on a school night and go to a bar or movie. It is legal to drink liquor at any age there.

> ### To Whom It May Concern
>
> "Genocide"
> Bourgeoisie!
> Beauty bending beside
> a wooden god,
> cursing and praying,
> Uttering together, like an
> Ancient chorus, along w/ the
> Sound of execution:
> Global Hope!
> Damp body,
> trampled every dawn
> —around six—
> walking nervously
> heading to work . . .
>
> —Manolis Pahakis

Manolis often writes poetry in his spare time.

ELLIS ISLA

Manolis Pahakis gets ready for a trip to the immigrant museum on Ellis Island, New York City.

Here after school I went to soccer practice from 3 to 6 P.M., then go home and cook for myself and study. Here I have to study harder because the language is different.

When I was in Greece I already knew about the racism in America. I heard about it on the television, from magazine articles. And you can see it here, even at this school, where blacks and whites often are in separate groups speaking poorly about one another. Some racism is directly related to economics. People who were born here are afraid their jobs will be taken by immigrants. Unfortunately we have this problem in Greece with the Albanian Greeks. They come from Albania, a poor country, and though they are ethnic Greeks they are discriminated against by the native Greeks. Many of these Albanian Greeks were sent back.

This may sound silly but I don't want to get married. I think I'm too weak to be in a marriage. It takes a lot of inner strength and confidence to make something so beautiful as a marriage work. I don't want to hurt myself and especially another person if I fail in this marriage.

The kids here are the same as in Iráklion, they are the same all over the world. They make jokes, love music, and enjoy life without worrying about things that will affect them when they become adults.

Living among other immigrants has many advantages and rewards. You learn about other cultures, become better educated, and that's what makes you a citizen of the world. The world is becoming like a small village. But this doesn't mean you should be separated from your own culture. Americans should keep their own culture and make an evolution into society where they keep their distinct identity while still being a vital member of that society.

> I love listening to old Greek music better than the modern Greek stuff that has no feeling in its music or song text. The modern stuff is just more commercial. My taste for American music is similar. I like the music of the fifties and sixties and jazz, especially be-bop.

Alina Girshovich

Age 16

Born in Riga, Latvia

Lives in Oradell, New Jersey

Alina Girshovich

> Movies and TV was my looking-glass into America. I imagined it to be Manhattan, everybody intelligent and nice.

I'm from Riga, Latvia. I came to the United States four and a half years ago. My parents wanted to come because they wanted more opportunities for themselves and for me and my sister. My parents are very honest people and earn money from their intelligence, and basically at that time in Russia, Latvia, if you didn't have a business or couldn't do something illegal, you wouldn't have any money. So they decided to come here and because of the discrimination against Jews in Latvia, they emigrated. I personally felt anti-Semitism myself.

I've become so used to my life here that I really don't remember how life was there that much. I remember missing my friends. It was weird when I came here. Everyone was different. Everyone would pick on us. I think that American kids are different a little bit, from Russian kids. They are different in personality, manners,… Maybe it's good, but I was shy. And I know that the kids who had just come to America were all quiet and shy. But American kids are more open, more outgoing, so basically that's why I and others felt picked on in the beginning.

When I first came here I was scared I guess, because everything seemed so…. It was a good experience I guess, a very different experience. Not everyone gets to move in their childhood to a completely different country. It has made me understand more things, made me stronger, more tolerant of others.

I think Russian young people are more independent than American kids, and more mature, definitely more mature. American kids they are…I guess it's because they depend on their parents too much. Because in Russia the high school was basically ten years. At sixteen years old a person has to pick, has to know what they want to be. If they want to be a doctor they go to medical school at sixteen. That's basically the difference, that's why they are more mature and independent. I think the earlier you become mature and independent the better. If you fool around too long it's not too good.

I really want to go back and visit someday. I really want to, because I know there are a lot of changes since I left. I really want to see this. But I definitely will not move back. Home will be America. The crucial years of my life, my teenage years, when I get used to stuff, I've spent here.

I've been playing the piano for eleven years. I started when I was five years

For recreation I go to the movies. I like comedy, and I saw Schindler's List, that had a tremendous effect on me. I think that it was a very wonderful movie. It effected me because my great-grandparents and their sisters and brothers were killed in the Holocaust.

old. I really enjoy playing, but I'm lazy, I don't practice too much. I don't know how I've managed to play concerts and do competitions, because I don't practice. I love classical music, but I'm lazy, I really am. I like to play, but not to practice.

On Sundays I go to my music school in Manhattan. I might go into music after high school and have that as my career, if everything goes fine and if I learn how to sit by the piano every day. Maybe I'll get into the Juilliard School program if I'm successful in music. I've also thought of being a lawyer, going to law school.

In Latvia, I wasn't aware of all the Jewish holidays. We still kept the tradition going but…basically what happened was my father's family was very religious. Well not very religious but at least they kept the traditions going. But my mother's family, her father was a very important figure in politics so he tried to suppress some of his Jewishness. He was a strong Communist. So because of that the Jewish religion and stuff was kind of kept down. But when I came here there were so many opportunities. First I went to a *yeshiva* (Jewish day school), and became familiar with my religion. I think every person should keep their religion going.

I think one of the biggest differences between high school kids here at River Dell High School and youth their same age in Russia is that here they're not familiar with the classics, with literature, with classical music, with everything that would make a person intelligent and well-rounded. I don't want to sound discriminating or that they are lowlifes, nothing like that, but basically their manners are less than what I expect a person to have.

They don't know classical music, they would rather listen to only the most popular styles of rock and roll. Now I'm sure there are these people in Russia too. If a Russian person were given the choice to go to a restaurant or to a concert, they would pick the concert. I mean most of the people would make that choice. But here it's basically the other way around. Here very few of my peers know classical musical or have read Dostoyevsky, Tolstoy, Faulkner for that matter.

I would tell another émigré my age coming from another country to be strong. To have respect for yourself. Not to give so much to what people will say, their comments. Not to forget your birthplace, your first homeland, not to be embarrassed.

Alina eats lunch with her friends at school.

Julia Kalashnikova

Age 16

Born in Tbilisi, Georgia

Lives in Oradell, New Jersey

Well I'm 50 percent Russian, or 75 percent because my father is pure Russian and my mother is half Armenian and half Greek. I lived in Georgia for about thirteen years, twelve, and then we moved down here.

Life was hard but it was fun, because you know we tried to make the best of it. My parents had good jobs so you know we had food on the table all the time. My mom was an engineer and my father he worked in the petroleum industry.

Tbilisi is a beautiful city, beautiful. Now it is all bombed because they had that war and it's just all horrible. I was there when the war was just starting and that is one of the reasons why we left, because of a lot of nationalism and stuff, because we weren't Georgian. At that time we couldn't go to Armenia because my father was Russian and people would pick on him and we couldn't go to Russia because my mother was Armenian. And it was just…there was nowhere to go.

Julia Kalashnikova works at Häagen-Dazs.

I don't like nationalism. I never liked it because I'm a mix of three cultures. And I had a lot of friends who were different nationalities and my parents never…we are a very mixed family. All my aunts and uncles are different so we are all mixed. It was really hard and very sad where I grew up, this was my home and I had to leave because some people just said you are not this nationality you can't live here, you can't be here.

My friends were sad to see me go. We all cried but a lot of my friends are here now in the United

States, which is good. My friends are all over the world. There are some in Israel, Greece, and Italy now. It was sad in the beginning. I was really upset, I cried every night. It was very hard to come here because I knew I wouldn't go back and probably never see all of my friends together again. I didn't know any English, I didn't speak a word of English. To not be able to hang out on the weekend, not to be able to communicate or ask do you want to hang out, or do you want to go shopping or do you want to go to the movies? I couldn't do that, so that was really hard.

I know how kids here are very judgmental especially in this area, very much so. God forbid you wear the same pair of jeans two days in a row, or God forbid a shirt or pullover. I think this is pathetic to be judged by your clothes and who you hang out with and what you wear. It was never like that in Georgia, because the life was harder so we matured kind of faster. We had to.

There really weren't that many possibilities for recreation in Georgia; we didn't have malls or big movie theaters where we could go. So we kind

---

I had totally expected this beautiful big country
and it is a wonderful country,
but it's not all that it's made out to be.

---

of made it all up. We were very creative. And we would do anything. We would go to someone's house, we would get together and sing, and we would have bonfires at night. I lived more toward the country so we had mountains and forests and we would go and make fires and bake potatoes. We would pick mushrooms—something I have been doing since I was little. I know the differences between the poisonous and nonpoisonous mushrooms because every summer me and my father went to pick mushrooms and my mom would marinate and bottle them. They were very good.

Meljunn Pascua

Age 16

Born in Famar, Philippines

Lives in Oradell, New Jersey

Meljunn Pascua

I was born in Famar, a mining town. I grew up there seven to eight years, then transferred to Zambales, a normal city.

I miss the Philippines a lot, especially my friends and the places we used to go to. We would go somewhere, cut classes sometimes. I don't do this here. We would go to the mountains, climb the trees, and get some fruit. All the guys waiting below for the fruit as you dropped it to them. I miss the nature of the Philippines, the mountains. I also miss my relatives. I haven't been back to visit since we moved but I'm thinking about visiting. But I have to earn money. I don't know if I would move back, but visiting I'm certain I'll do. I don't know about staying permanently, because my family and most of my relatives are here, so I'll probably stay here.

We moved to be here with my father. My father was a permanent resident in the U.S. so we wanted to join my father. We hadn't seen him for eight years, so we just transferred here to be with him. I really missed my dad, it was too many years not being able to hold him.

The first thing that was hard for me when I came to America was making friends and getting along with the weather, because in the Philippines it is really hot. Life is different here because of the people and the different language. And the places, the locations.... In the Philippines I knew a lot of the places; here where I transferred I know nothing. That's about it. Places, people—getting along with them, that's about it.

> When I lived in the Philippines, I thought living in America was easy. I thought it was a normal life but with different people. The biggest shock for me was the language.

We can speak a lot of languages in the Philippines. We grow up and learn how to use these languages. I was surprised to meet many students here who only knew one language. Knowing only one language is kind of limiting.

In my free time, I enjoy doing track. Next season I'm going to participate in track. I joined the wrestling team two years ago. I like it. It gets me into shape and keeps me in shape. And that's about it. Every day, up to Saturday, I practice wrestling. Saturdays after wrestling and on Sundays I go to work. I work at Foodtown. I've been working there almost a year. The job is not my favorite but I'm earning money. Some of the money I earn goes to the bank and some of it goes to my family, for house's expenses like groceries. I don't mind sharing with them, I'm part of the family.

I like medicine and thought about becoming a doctor but we can't afford it, it's too expensive, so I'll go to nursing instead. Maybe I'll get a scholarship, I hope, I wish, and from nursing I can go on to study becoming a doctor. This is what I'm thinking.

Just be yourself. Don't copy anyone, just be yourself. Don't mind them if they tell you stuff, just don't mind them. Don't get in trouble. Be yourself, enjoy yourself, that's it.

Meljunn gets a workout at wrestling practice.

Ai Hirono

Age 16

Born in Tokyo, Japan

Lives in Oradell, New Jersey

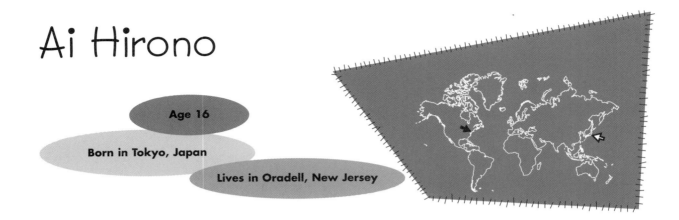

I was born in Tokyo, but I don't remember much about the place because we moved when I was three. I lived in Djakarta, Indonesia, for five years. We moved because of my dad's business, which is a trading company.

I liked Djakarta, but it wasn't a neat city, it was quite dirty. You couldn't walk around in the night, even in the morning because it was very dangerous. We always needed a driver because my mom doesn't drive. We had two drivers and two women that worked for us, cleaning, cooking, and everything else for us. This part of life in Djakarta was nice.

After Djakarta, we moved back to Tokyo, when I was in third grade. Because Djakarta is a hot place with a lot of sunshine, my skin was very dark. When we came back to Japan it was winter and everyone was staring at me because I was so dark, my dark skin. That was bit strange.

We came to America two years ago, because of my dad's business. We are going to stay here for five years, then move back to Japan. My father said he would send me to college anywhere I want to go, but I think I'll go to college in Japan.

I miss Japan. Sometimes I miss my friends especially. The houses here are much bigger. There are a lot more parks here, a lot more green. In Tokyo we lived in an apartment. There are no plants, no trees. I don't especially enjoy seeing all this green. I love my apartment. I loved living in a tall building. Some people feel it is important to have free spaces near where they live, but not me.

Ai Hirono

I like listening to soft rock, not rap. I don't know the groups by their name. I just listened to what I like on TV, on VH-1.

The biggest difficulty for me adjusting to American culture has been the language and having a friend. I didn't care about my grades in school, I only wanted my friends. Now I'm very happy because I have some good friends. If I didn't have this I would want to go back to Japan more. Friendship is especially important for me.

When I first came here to New Jersey everyone made fun of me because of my name Ai, but I didn't care, I know they didn't mean it. I was glad that they recognized my name as different, not a usual one like Susan, Terry, or Bill, because Ai is unique here in America.

I think there is a little discrimination of Orientals here in America. It doesn't matter if some-one comes from Russia, India, or America, but the students look at all Asians as Oriental—the same even if we come from Japan, Korea or China. They think there is a country named Oriental. They look at us differently and this doesn't make me feel good. I try not to think that I'm Oriental. I am Oriental and I'm proud of it, too. They say certain things like all Oriental people are smart in math, Orientals only study, can't do anything but study and we all have a lot of money. Most of these things have some truth to them but I don't know, I don't want them to say it. We didn't come here searching for money. It doesn't matter if we have money, or knowl-edge, we just want to live here because we want to. I don't want to talk about money with my friends, it's my parents' business.

Oriental people wear clothes a little differently, but I don't like this. Now I'm dressed more like an American teenager. In the suburbs in Japan the young people wear short pants, with Mickey on them, they wear a two-dollar or three-dollar T-shirt and a necklace that says Love on it. I don't like this at all,

My Town

My town had a voice.
That nostalgic feeling . . . when downtown
  scenes appear in movies and novels:
the good, strong voice of the greengrocer
  calling customers,
the housewives heedlessly caught up in
  chatter,
children emerging from the public bath—
  all shouting,
each louder than the next, as they await
  their parents' arrival to pick them up.
The smoke of fish roasting tells the hour.
Junior high and high school kids quickly
  pedaling their bicycles
back from school club meetings,
and the lights of the shopping district
  burning.
Businessmen bustling homeward.

It could give vitality to its people,
while enwrapped in a package of every-
  day peace and gentleness—my town had
  that power.

Now, still, in the town I left,
there are surely some who feel that
  powerful and peaceful warmth.
Somewhere in that town, surely.

Ai Hirono

Ai feels that sometimes it's easier to express herself in poetry.

SIZE: 377,765 square kilometers (145,856 square miles), slightly smaller than California
POPULATION: 126 million
CAPITAL: Tokyo (population 8.25 million)
ETHNICITIES: Japanese, Korean, Chinese, Ainu
RELIGIONS: Shintoism, Buddhism, Christianity
LANGUAGES: Japanese, Korean
MONETARY UNIT: yen
TRADITIONAL FOODS: sushi, tempura (deep fried vegetables or seafood), tsukemono (pickled vegetables)
INTERNATIONALLY KNOWN JAPANESE: Hideo Nomo (L.A. Dodgers' pitcher), Yoko Ono (singer/songwriter), Seijei Ozawa (orchestra conductor), Yo-Yo Ma (cellist), Midori (violinist), Akira Kurosawa (film director)
✱ With 13,765 people per square mile, Japan is one of the most densely populated nations in the world. The Tokyo Stock Exchange is the largest in the world in total value of transactions handled.

I think freedom is something one must earn from society, it is not to be expected just because you exist.

this sameness. They all have the same haircuts, bobbed with a clip in their hair. I don't like those Oriental ways. I will not dress this way when I return to Japan. That is why I cut my hair. There were no short-haired people in this school and I don't want to be like everyone else.

I don't hang out with other Japanese students much here in school, or speak Japanese. Speaking Japanese isn't going to help me.

If I speak English this will help me learn the language. We are living here and we have to learn English. This is our purpose here, to learn English. I'm not thinking about my Japanese culture while I'm here in America. Now I'm in this country so English should be my first language.

I don't believe in God. My parents don't have any religion and neither do I, we have nothing. During religious holidays we take a trip, take a vacation. We don't believe in God or in any kind of supernatural being. Most Japanese people still have a Christmas tree and celebrate the holiday as a world holiday, just to have something to celebrate, to have a good time. We don't think about Christmas being the birthday of Jesus, just that it is Christmas, no school, no work.

Only a few people use drugs in Japan, but it's not a big problem like it is here. We have another problem, harassment in school, harassing students. This is when five or six people beat up one person. They are not gangs, they just beat up this person because this person did something wrong. If this person does something different others are going to beat him. This month in Japan, three kids committed suicide because of harassment. We had a kid who was beat up in our school, too. In Japan we feel everyone has to do the same, be homogenous. If a kid lives in a poor apartment and cannot afford good clothes people are going to beat him up. I know it doesn't make sense to you because you are an American. This is not right but I think this is part of our culture. We can't help it, we have lived in a country for over three thousand years that celebrates sameness for the good of the country. I even chased a boy with some other friends because he was not so smart in his studies. This is not right, but it just is.

Vica Berman

Age 11

Born in Mukachevo, Ukraine

Lives in Sarasota, Florida

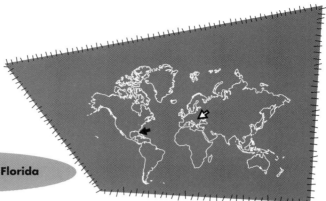

Vica Berman relaxes at home.

I was born in Mukachevo, Ukraine. Life was good there. I went to school, went to the synagogue, played with my friends and watched TV. We had an Alfa television, a good one.

Mukachevo isn't really a big city, but it has houses like here in Sarasota. I miss everything there, especially my friends and school and the way of living. People were more true, more real when they said good morning to you, not like here, where it often seems the adults say things to you without really meaning it.

School is different, too. Well, here I'm in the fifth grade and I'm learning something like 232 times 8, something like that. In Mukachevo I did this in second grade. I'm learning this material twice and it is very boring. I would like to have higher math but I don't think they have it at my school.

After school I go outside and ride my bike or stay home and watch TV, or I go to sleep if I want to or read some books. I love reading books about dogs. My favorite dog is the collie, like

> I found out America isn't exactly what I was told it would be like. It's ok, but I miss my country.

Lassie. I would like to become a veterinarian because I love animals. In Mukachevo I had a cat, my grandma had a cat and my big sister had a dog.

I have no friends here. Well I should be honest, I do have one friend who lives in this building. In my country I could make friends very easily. On my birthday in my country I had nineteen people over and here I just had one, and she was a Russian girl.

We eat Russian food and speak Russian in our home. I don't think I can forget to speak and read Russian, but sometimes when I am writing in Russian I write an American letter between the Russian letters. I will never forget to speak Russian, it is who I am. I want to be able to explain myself to my people in the language I was born into. The first language my ears heard.

In school one girl said I smoked because I'm Russian and because I'm stupid. I couldn't say anything to her. She thinks Russian people are stupid. We don't know how to talk, we wear only old clothes, we live in a country that has only cold weather, we are all poor and all of us drink vodka. Sometimes my classmates ask me to speak Russian because they think it sounds strange.

> Sometimes I like to listen to music like my sister, like Nirvana and Guns N' Roses. I heard this in Mukachevo as well, I had to listen to this kind of music because this is what my sister liked. But I sometimes listened to Russian and Hungarian music too.

One of the biggest differences between Mukachevo and Sarasota is summer, it is much hotter here and there is no snow here in wintertime. There are no palms in Ukraine, we have different kinds of trees. Here the grass is like carpet, like plastic. In my country grass is green like it is supposed to be, but there is nothing underneath it, just the dirt.

I like to play basketball sometimes but I don't like to dance because I usually trip over my feet. But my big sister—I have two older sisters, actually, and both are good dancers. Perhaps when I am their age I will be more used to America and its strange ways.

UKRAINE

SIZE: 603,703 square kilometers (233,090 square miles), about the size of Texas

POPULATION: 52,393,000

CAPITAL: Kyyiv (Kiev) (population 2,700,000)

ETHNICITIES: Ukrainian, Russian, Jewish, Belarusian, Polish, Hungarian, Bulgarian, Moldavian, Rom (Gypsy)

RELIGIONS: Christianity (Ukrainian Orthodox, Russian Orthodox, Greek Catholic, Baptists), Judaism

LANGUAGES: Ukrainian, Russian, Belorusian, Polish, Hungarian

MONETARY UNIT: hryvna

BECAME INDEPENDENT: August 24, 1991

TRADITIONAL FOODS: borscht (beet soup), varenyky (stuffed, boiled dumplings), holubtsi (stuffed cabbage)

INTERNATIONALLY KNOWN UKRAINIANS: Taras Sherchenko (literary figure and patriot), Alexandr Dorzhenko (film director), Viktor Petrenko and Oksana Baiul (Olympic gold medalists in ice skating)

✱ The largest nuclear disaster ever happened in Chernobyl, Ukraine in April 1986.

Marwa abou El-Ella

Age 13

Born in Al-Farwānīyah, Kuwait

Lives in Dearborn, Michigan

I came here seven months ago. I was born in Kuwait, then we moved after nine years to Egypt. My mother is Egyptian and my father is Palestinian. I liked both countries but I feel as a Palestinian.

We had to come here because Egypt wouldn't let my father stay because he is Palestinian. We came here so I could get my citizenship, then I will move back to Egypt and finish school there, Shi-Allah [If Allah wishes it to be].

School was easier in Kuwait than here because I knew the language. I could read the books. The language, English, is coming to me, slowly, but it is coming. Now I have American and Arabic friends.

School was hard in Egypt. There I was learning math, science, language, arts, French, social studies, and Arabic. I like Egypt very much.

After school if I don't come to ACCESS [Arab Community Center for Economic and Social Services], then I study for my tests, do my writing, read stories in Arabic and English, and do my math. I don't play out in the street. This is not proper for an Arabic girl.

In Egypt I would go to the park and play with my relatives. I have uncles and aunts that live there. They have many children, so I have many cousins. I have no family in Kuwait, only in Egypt and in Jordan. I would like to go to Palestine and see where my father was born. He comes from a village on the West Bank. I hope Palestine will become a country like the other countries that you read about in the United Nations.

Marwa abou El-Ella sits in back of the ACCESS building, not far from the smokestacks of Henry Ford's first automobile factory.

*Marwa hugs her friend
Laila Mawari.*

When I was in Kuwait and Egypt I heard there
were many bad things in America.

I have two brothers and three sisters. My brother who is finishing college can't come here because we don't have the citizenship papers, only the green cards. He and my sister, she is married, are studying the sciences and computers. I have two sisters, the youngest and oldest, who live with me in Dearborn.

My father was a science teacher for four years but he doesn't work now, neither does my mother. My older sister works in some kind of office job and helps with the money of our home. I want to be either a children's doctor or a teeth doctor. I have always been interested in the sciences.

I wear the *massar* [scarf, headcover] because I want to wear it. But there are Arabic girls who don't wear it. It isn't *haram* [forbidden] if you don't wear it. What is *haram* is if you wear the *massar* and then you take it off in public sometimes. You either wear it all the time or you don't ever wear it.

I like Dearborn but I don't like the big Ford car factory. So much smoke is coming from the chimneys and it causes you to cough and breathe in dirty air. This pollution could give you some diseases.

I like America and Dearborn very much. Here in Dearborn we are many Muslims. It is like a small Arabic village. If you want you can speak only Arabic the whole day with no problems.

There are American people who don't like Arabic people. They don't understand our culture and religion. They say we are different, speak a different language, eat different food, so we can't be trusted. Then there are some Arabic kids in my school who swear to some American students, which is *haram*. These students get angry because they don't understand what was said in Arabic. This is not good either. In my class I have some good American students and I have some Arabic students who I don't like.

I like Arabic and American food. When I go to McDonald's I can eat if I want the hamburger because it isn't pork, but I choose not to. This meat is not *halal* [prepared according to Islamic dietary rules]. I can eat pizza or fish sandwiches in restaurants when I eat out. We rarely eat out because it is too expensive and my mother's cooking tastes better.

Laila Mawari

Age 13

Born in San'a, Yemen

Lives in Dearborn, Michigan

I came to Dearborn in 1992. My father brought us here. He had been here already for ten years. I had never seen my father. When I arrived in Dearborn was the first time in my life I met my father.

He told me I will stay here and finish college and become a doctor. I want to be a doctor. I like helping other people who are in pain and in need of a remedy.

I live with my father, stepmother, three brothers, and little sister. I have an older sister who is married and lives in another house near us.

I have cousins and my mother in San'a and I miss her big time. She is the one who took care of me my first ten years. She helped me in school and cared for me when I was sick. I call her once every month and write her every two weeks. She lives with her sister, who is also divorced. I also miss my friends. I had such close friends that when I think about them it makes me sad.

The nature in Yemen is quite different from the Detroit area. We have beautiful mountains which look purple at sundown because of the light and shadows cast upon them. The air is fresher in San'a, much fresher.

In San'a if I didn't know my multiplication table by heart, they would take a stick, an *assa* in Arabic, and hit me on the head hard. The boys would get hit on their feet. This is a custom that should be changed there. I have learned no less or slower here than when I was in school in

Laila lives in the Muslim section of Dearborn, the largest Arabic community in the United States.

Marwa and Laila stand near the mosque in Dearborn.

San'a. The threat of getting hit by the stick didn't make me learn more. School in Dearborn is much better because of this reason.

The American girls go to the movies or to the malls with boys, or by themselves without their mothers. In Yemen our tradition is for the girl to be with the mother until she is married. I have no interest in going out by myself, no way.

I don't even want to get married, but if I don't it is considered *haram*, forbidden by Allah. I'll get married when I'm old, when I'm in my twenties, have finished medical school, and have my own home. It is my choice who I want to marry. I will marry an Arab, a Yemeni, no way a Jewish man. If I married an Egyptian man and we get divorced he'll say he wants the kids in Egypt. He'll remarry an Egyptian woman and my kids will forget the Yemeni culture. Only a Yemeni for me.

Girls and boys were in one classroom when I first came here. When we would go to lunch or go

OFFICIAL NAME:
Republic of Yemen

SIZE: 122,310 square
kilometers (203,850 miles),
about the size of Nevada and
Montana combined

POPULATION: 13,897,000

CAPITAL: San'a
(population 237,016)

ETHNICITY: Arab

RELIGION: Islam

LANGUAGE: Arabic

MONETARY UNIT: rial

TRADITIONAL FOODS:
m'lawakh (fried flat bread),
hilbba (a kind of whipped
cream used in soups), kh'ell
(cardomon used in coffee)

**INTERNATIONALLY
KNOWN YEMENIS:**
Ofra Haza (pop singer),
Abdalla Albradoni (poet)

✱ Yemen is one of the oldest
centers of Western civilization in
the Near East. Yemen was ruled
by several empires, the last two
being the Ottoman Turks (North
Yemen) and the British (South
Yemen, sometimes known as
Aden). The two Yemens united
on May 22, 1990.

outside during recess they would make fun of us. They think that someone who doesn't speak English is a "boater." They don't hang around him, or play with him. Even the Arab-Americans, they called me "boater." This treatment made me feel bad. Learning English was easy. I learned it fast, so I was a "boater" for only a short time. But now all that has stopped because I speak English. I decided that if a new girl comes to our classroom I'll hang around her even if she is a "boater." I won't care what others will say, I'll hang with her still.

Some boys and girls made fun of my *massar*—the scarf I wear around my head—but I didn't

> I haven't seen many movies, only two. I saw The Mario Bros. and The Little Mermaid.

care. This is our culture, the Muslim way of dressing. One must be proud of her culture and religion no matter how different it may seem to others. You begin wearing it when you are seven. You are not supposed to show your hair, a sign of beauty, to anyone except your husband.

I don't see myself moving back to San'a. I will visit, however. I want to bring my mom back here so we can live together. But who knows what will happen?

Here life is much easier for me than it was in Yemen. I can go to the park or come here to ACCESS and be with my friends. But in Yemen I can't go anywhere. It is more strict for the girls. I have less freedom there. It is more boring there, but I like my country and would like to visit.

Irina Tsyrkina

Age 13

Born in Borisov, Belarus

Lives in Skokie, Illinois

We left Borisov in 1991 for many reasons. We left because of religious persecution, we are Jewish. Also my mom needed surgery on her leg and my dad's relatives were all here. About three months before we left I noticed kids didn't play with me anymore. Their parents told them not to play with me because I was Jewish.

When we came here we didn't have any money, no jobs, and didn't know the language. It was especially hard for my sister, she was sixteen and had left everything there. She would cry every day for several months. I still miss my friends, school, and teacher. My father is now a part-time manager of a parking garage, he'll soon be the manager. In Borisov, he was in the army and had a high rank.

We wore uniforms at school in Belarus and went every day except for Sundays. We went to school in shifts. My shift was from 1:30 to 6 P.M. Every year your shift changed.

Math is so easy here. What I am learning now in the eighth grade, I learned in Borisov in the fourth grade. In Belarus, the students are more disciplined than here. Girls never wore nail polish to school or bangs in their faces. They couldn't wear makeup or anything like that.

I liked it better in the schools in Belarus, particularly the disciplinary rules. I don't think it's

Irina Tsyrkina

Irina stands in front of her home with her uncle, aunt, and father.

necessary for girls to wear makeup to school. They will have the rest of their lives to alter their looks from what Mother Nature gave them.

I was able to learn the language fairly quickly. I had no choice. I had to communicate with others, read books, and watch TV. When we first came here my parents sent me to a Jewish school and I really got into it. Because I hadn't learned anything in Belarus about my religion I was really interested in it. My parents got scared because they thought I was becoming Orthodox. I still go sometimes to the synagogue but I'm not religious. Both synagogues I went to were burned down here in Skokie. They think the kids who did it were white kids, like Nazis.

When I'm not studying I read, draw, watch TV, and go to parties with my parents on the weekends. I used to collect stamps but not anymore. I have many old stamps so if I sold the collection I'd probably get a lot of money. I also like to draw designs for women's clothing. I want to be a pediatrician and have a business designing clothes.

I absolutely will go back and visit Borisov, even though my parents don't want to return. This is where my most important childhood memories were formed. My grandparents and great-grandparents were born there and are buried there. I would visit the cemetery to let them know we haven't forgotten them, and visit my teachers if they haven't retired yet.

I love Russian classical music and music like Boyz II Men, that kind of music, slow songs. I'm not really interested in movies so I rarely go.

OFFICIAL NAME:
Republic of Belarus
SIZE: 207,640 square kilometers (80,130 square miles), a little bigger than Kansas
POPULATION: 10,310,000
CAPITAL: Minsk
(population 1,633,000)
ETHNICITIES: Belarusian, Russian, Ukrainian, Polish, Jewish, Rom (Gypsy)
RELIGIONS: Christianity (Eastern Orthodox, Roman Catholic), Judaism
LANGUAGES: Belarusian, Ukrainian, Russian, Polish
MONETARY UNIT: ruble
BECAME INDEPENDENT:
December 18, 1991
TRADITIONAL FOODS:
draniki (potato pancake), machanka (hot cereal made with pork pieces and onion)
INTERNATIONALLY KNOWN BELARUSIANS:
Vitaly Scherbo (Olympic gymnast), Natalia Zvereva (pro tennis player)
✳ Minsk, the capital city, was founded in the eleventh century as a major commercial center on the rail link between Moscow and Warsaw.

I speak Russian and English at home. But if I say something in English to my mother she will not answer me unless I repeat it in Russian. She was a Russian language teacher in Belarus and is very proud of the language and literature. I used to speak some Belarusian, they were just beginning to teach it in the schools after we became independent.

I think America should always leave its doors open to immigrants because America is a country founded on immigration. Only the native Americans have the right to say something about foreigners.

I really had no ideas about America before I came. I was just coming with my parents and I

> In winter at home we couldn't eat strawberries, here we can.

didn't have any time to think about our move. The biggest shock to me was the stores that had so many kinds of food here.

I think people should stop being prejudiced and not judge people by their color or the way they look but by what they really are inside.

I would like to marry someone who would understand me, know what it was for me when I came here and people were already judging me. I would teach him Russian so when we have holidays or parties he would be able to understand and participate in the conversation. I would like to maintain and practice my religion so I would prefer to marry a Jew. I would tell my children to be proud of their religion. Not like when I was young in Borisov, where I didn't know I was Jewish until the age of eight.

Irina writes "This is a picture of a woman telling her daughter that she can't be my friend, because I am Jewish."

Marian Reyes

Age 14

Born in Bulalacao, Philippines

Lives in Skokie, Illinois

I came from a small town near Manila, called Bulalacao. Living in Bulalacao was like living in the country. My father raised chickens and roosters. He sold the eggs to different people trying to breed strong new breeds. These chickens and roosters are used for the sport of cockfighting. He doesn't breed them now since he is living here. His cousin does it for him back in the Philippines.

Cockfighting is kind of exciting but when they die it's kind of sad. It's kind of like a horse race. You go to this place, a kind of arena, and you place bets on the roosters you think will win their fights. Mostly men go, but I was allowed to attend because my father was one of the owners and breeders.

We lived in a ranch house, where a river with fish ran behind our home. The topography of the land was very different there than in Skokie, because we also had mountains behind our home. There it is usually hot and humid most of the time, you are often sweaty. Here you get to experience the different seasons which effects you both physically and spiritually.

I miss my friends in Bulalacao and I write to them once a month in Tagalog. We speak this language at home, too. My dad told us not to forget the language because when we go home we'll need to speak in Tagalog with friends and family so we can understand each other.

After I was born my mother moved here to Chicago to find a better job. She is a nurse at

Marian Reyes

Lakeshore Hospital. She then petitioned for us to join her here in America, so my dad could get a better job and we could get a better education. I had been living without my mother for eight years, being raised by my grandmother. I was used to her and I didn't want to leave. I was crying when we left. I had this plan that when we were all ready to leave I would hide in a cardboard box so they couldn't find me. It's strange now. Because of the distance I don't miss her as much and don't write her. It's kind of weird.

I don't really miss much of the culture. However, when I came here it was difficult because I didn't know how I would communicate since I didn't know any English. Once the phone was ringing and I didn't want to answer it because

> My image of America before I came here was based upon the postcards my mom would send to me. There were these beautiful lakes and mountains.

what would I say. I began to sweat. Luckily it was another Filipino friend so we could speak Tagalog. Language was my main concern.

Meeting friends was not too difficult, but I want to lose my accent. Some of my friends say, and not in a mean way, "Oh, you speak kind of funny," so I've thought of trying to acquire an American accent, a midwestern accent. I think it's cool to be friends with all kinds of kids from different cultures. I have an Indian friend, a Russian and Syrian friends. I think knowing and living among different groups of people prepares a child better for the adult world.

We still cook Filipino food at home, lots of fried rice and egg rolls. My mom makes a dish called "adobo," beef sliced up into little squares with soy sauce. Adjusting to my home here hasn't been hard but for my parents it was more difficult. My father works at a bank in the checking department working with computers. I'm used to American culture now. I'm used to easy money here. Items are cheaper here.

When I first attended school here I thought all of the work was easy because we were more advanced back home. Only American history, the Constitution was hard because at home we learned Filipino history and I knew nothing of American history.

My normal day after school is do my homework, watch TV, eat, watch some more TV, and go to bed. We don't go out much. I've only seen three movies since we came here five years ago. I do have two hobbies which are singing in the Music Club after school and taking tae kwon do classes. I do exercise my mind and body a little, despite my addiction to the TV.

My parents want me to be a doctor and I guess I want to be a doctor for kids, or possibly an archi-

Marian and Irina Tsyrkina pose with their classmates.

tect for homes. I like drawing and designing homes. If being an architect makes a lot of money, I guess they'll let me go for it.

I would tell a girl my age coming to America from the Philippines to follow and maintain her culture. Be yourself and don't follow people who you think are going to be a bad influence. Don't hang with people who smoke, use drugs, or drink liquor. If I did this my parents would kill me. Unfortunately, those young people doing this stuff are making their future bleak.

Ruenjai Phengphipat

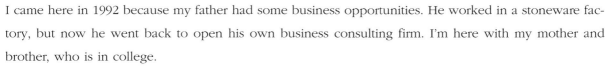

Age 16

Born in Bangkok, Thailand

Lives in Deerfield, Illinois

I came here in 1992 because my father had some business opportunities. He worked in a stoneware factory, but now he went back to open his own business consulting firm. I'm here with my mother and brother, who is in college.

I am planning on returning to Thailand when I graduate here. I will go to college in Bangkok. I will study business finance. I miss my dad and want to be with him. I'll return to the United States for

Ruenjai Phengphipat

my master's degree. When I return maybe I'll stay here with my mom. She likes it here because it is quiet so she'll remain. But I should add we are pretty comfortable in both places so our plans are flexible for the future.

I visited Bangkok last summer. I thought I would really miss it. But the city was full of traffic, air pollution, noise, and bad weather, so I didn't really enjoy it that much. I miss my friends and it is my country so I'll return anyway.

High school in Bangkok is very different from here at Deerfield High. First and foremost you don't have any choices of subjects in Bangkok. Here you have so many choices and levels to choose from. In Thailand if you are in a math class and the level is too difficult for you, it's too bad, you'll just get a bad grade on your report card. Here they try to put you in classes according to your ability. I think being able to take varying classes better prepares you for college and life in general. The world outside isn't just made up of one kind of math, science, and literature.

Most people say that it is easier here but I don't think so. I'm taking the highest-level courses and all in English so it is quite difficult for me, but I'm managing. Sometimes I don't get to bed until 3 A.M. because I'm studying.

I began playing the violin seven years ago. But because I had so much homework, I didn't have time to practice and I really didn't have a teacher who motivated me. Here at this school I really enjoy playing in the orchestra. I was motivated to practice because when the conductor would ask us to play by ourselves I would be embarrassed if I sounded terrible. I received the most improvement award in the eighth and ninth grades because I really practiced.

When I'm not doing homework, I'm practicing my violin and on the weekends baby-sitting. I have seven families I baby-sit for and it is good money. I still don't feel that comfortable with the language so I don't go out to the movies or other places with my friends. It's hard to explain. Plus when I go clothes shopping with my mom she pays, so I prefer shopping with her than my friends.

At first I hated it here. I knew a lot of people but none of them were really friends. I'm kind of shy so it was difficult to meet other kids. It's hard for me to explain, but being the only Thai student at this school didn't help matters. There are

> I think American-born kids should take the time to visit other countries so they will see how difficult it is to live.

very few foreign students at this school, maybe because it is in the suburbs. I know that in the city of Chicago there are many foreign kids going to school.

I've never really had a problem here with other kids bothering me because I'm Thai. Maybe some say things about my accent but I just laugh with them. The kids who are the nicest to me are those who have traveled to other lands. Travel is a great equalizer and can humble the biggest of people. Some people say there are too many immigrants coming to the U.S. Some cities have too many and these people need to move to states like Nebraska, Wyoming, or Montana, where the immigrant population is much smaller.

I think it is a good thing that the U.S. allows people from different countries to study here. I want to return to my country so I can improve it. My real goal in life is to become the prime minister in Thailand. Becoming prime minister will not be easy because women in Thailand are not treated as equally as they are treated here. It is still a very male-domineering society.

If other countries developed strong economies and democratic governments then not as many people will leave their homelands. It is not American culture that attracts foreigners to this country, but the many opportunities to improve the quality of life. People choose a restaurant not for its decor or price so much as for the many choices on the menu and the high quality of food.

Coming here has made me learn so many new things. I am more mature now. When I visit my friends in Bangkok they say I seem older, not like a kid anymore. Since my mother doesn't speak much English I have been the one to take care of myself outside the home.

A lot of the rich Thai kids in Bangkok try to be like Americans, dressing like them, singing their music. Probably the greatest influence on kids today outside of America is MTV. We watch and want to either become like these people on MTV or at least experience some of what they are doing. I call MTV Manic Tunnel Vision, because after watching it all you have on your brain is the music, clothes, dance, and sex.

THAILAND

OFFICIAL NAME:
Kingdom of Thailand
SIZE: 513,115 square kilometers (198,114 square miles) about the size of Texas
POPULATION: 58,265,000
CAPITAL: Bangkok (population 5,572,712)
ETHNICITIES: Thai, Chinese, Malay, Lisu, Luwa, Shan, Karen, Vietnamese
RELIGIONS: Buddhism, Islam
LANGUAGES: Thai and regional dialects
MONETARY UNIT: baht
TRADITIONAL FOODS: tapioca, pan fried noodles, phat thai (mixed shrimp and noodles)
INTERNATIONALLY KNOWN THAIS: Dok Mai Sot, Si Burapha (novelists)
✱ Thai date the founding of their nation to the year 1238, when a Thai chieftain overthrew Khmer State of Angkor at Sukhathai and established the kingdom. The name of the country until 1939 was Kingdom of Siam.

José Salvador Cotto

Age 14

Born in San Salvador, El Salvador

Lives in South San Francisco, California

I came here three years ago to better my education and begin a new life. I came with my brother. My father is here now but my mother and four brothers are still in San Salvador. My father works as a janitor at the airport. My country is small and poor so my father sends money to my mother.

El Salvador is a small beautiful country made up of fourteen states, but it is too hot and humid there all the time. I think because the weather isn't so hot here I'm hungrier. We eat many of the same foods here as we did in San Salvador, except Mom isn't cooking the food. I love tamales, pupusas, and pasteles.

José Salvador Cotto

I do miss my family, friends, school, and especially my little brother. School was no harder or easier in my country, the only difference is I have to learn in English.

You hear that everything is going to be great but it's not that great. This is probably true for most countries. One probably fantasizes about a place and people based upon books, magazines, and especially movies because it is so visual. But reality is never the

We learned about America through the movies. <u>Robocop</u>, <u>Rambo</u>, and others.

same as fantasy. Maybe that's why the word fantastic comes from the word fantasy. Aren't all fantasies fantastic? The reality is there are too many gangs here. If they stayed to themselves okay, but when they bother you, try to get you to join them, then they are no good.

Math is my favorite subject here in school. Math should help me when I go to college to learn about designing cars. I want to be a car designer.

EL SALVADOR

OFFICIAL NAME:
Republic of El Salvador
SIZE: 21,476 square kilometers
(8,260 miles), about the size of
Massachusetts
POPULATION: 5,768,000
CAPITAL: San Salvador
(population 435,000)
ETHNICITIES: Mestizo,
Indian, Caucasian
RELIGIONS: Christianity
(Roman Catholic, Protestant)
LANGUAGES: Spanish,
Nahua (Indian language)
MONETARY UNIT: colon
**BECAME
INDEPENDENT:**
September 15, 1821
TRADITIONAL FOODS:
Pupusas (corn pancakes enfold-
ing cheese, beans, or meat)
**INTERNATIONALLY
KNOWN EL
SALVADORANS:** Augustio
Farabundo Martí (political
activist), Alberto Masgerrer
(writer), Francisco Gavidia
(philosopher, historian, writer)
✽ Mesoamericans like the
Mayans, Lenca and Pipil
inhabited the area of modern
El Salvador long before the
16th century Spanish conquest.

I don't understand all this talk about illegal aliens, they are taking our jobs away and everything else. Did the Pilgrims have visas? Did the colonists coming from England in the days of Ben Franklin have green cards?

These immigrants do work. They usually do the work most Americans find too difficult or boring. Why discriminate against these people? When I see the news on TV about things like this, like Proposition 187, you don't see them talking about white South Africans, Polish people, or Irish people. These people have what in common, their skin color, meaning they are not brown or black.

Our Spanish is similar to that in Mexico, Puerto Rico, Colombia, but they have some words that they only say, just like we have some we only say. I guess it is like the English spoken in Alabama is probably a little different from the English spoken in Oregon, just a few words, you know some slang, things like that.

I would tell another El Salvadoran who is my age coming to America not to feel bad just because he doesn't speak English. You will learn to take some time and effort but be patient. Watch TV programs, like cartoons and music videos, these will help you learn quicker. Be patient like a goalie in a soccer game. Soon the ball will be coming towards you and you'll have to defend the goal.

José competes in a soccer game after school.

I love rap, rock and roll, pop, and music from my country, cumbias, a kind of dancing music. I like Guns N' Roses, Mariah Carey, and the Black Crowes.

Doreen Chand

Age 12

Born in Suva, Fiji

Lives in South San Francisco, California

We came here to be with my mom's sisters, brothers, mother, and grandpa. My mom works in the Hyatt Hotel housekeeping and my dad works in a store. He doesn't live with us. I see him almost every week.

It was really nice living in Fiji. Almost every weekend we would go to the beach and swim in the warm ocean. Most of my free time was spent swimming or building sand castles.

In Fiji I spoke Hindi at home, but here in South San Francisco I speak mostly English. I'm forgetting Hindi. I know it's important to remember your first language but everywhere I hear and use English even at home. My ancestors come from India and on Fiji we used to go to a Hindu temple. We used to walk up this mountain through beautiful tall trees and wildflowers. The temple was built out of very large stones. We would say our prayers and then offer some gifts, like food, to the Hindu God.

I left the island when I was seven years old so it wasn't too hard to leave, I was very young. But I still miss my friends and the ocean. Here the water is always cold. Living on Fiji we didn't have as much air pollution or noises from cars. It was much cleaner than South San Francisco.

In Fiji we always

Doreen Chand points to Fiji on a map.

Life seemed slower and lazier there. Here everyone drives fast, honks his horn, and walks in a hurry.

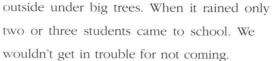

wore uniforms in school. Our school was outside. We would learn sitting outside under big trees. When it rained only two or three students came to school. We wouldn't get in trouble for not coming.

Doreen remembers her homeland through her artwork.

My favorite subject in school is art. When I'll finish school I want to be a kindergarten teacher because I like small children.

I like most everything here except the violence. Once we were visiting my grandma in San Bruno and we heard about this maniac who was going around with a knife stabbing people. We heard this on the news. Immediately my grandma made us come in the house. Now we can't go skating around her home unless she watches us and can see us at all times. We didn't have this kind of violence in Fiji. Maybe there is more violence here because there are many different kinds of people who don't listen to or respect each other.

I like living in a country that has many different kinds of people because you can learn about their cultures, learn their languages, and eat some great food. In Fiji they eat more beans and potatoes and food is much spicier. Sometimes I eat food so spicy, so hot my nose runs.

We celebrate here the American holidays like Christmas but not Halloween. One of our Hindi holidays is called Deepanile (Festival of Lights). You eat no meat and pray to Ram (God). You aren't supposed to play outside, especially girls with long hair, because God lets the devil out to catch you. My friend's mom was captured by the devil and it took a special kind of religious doctor to cure her.

Doreen has a laugh during lunch at school.

Alexander Collazos

Age 13

Born in Lima, Peru

Lives in South San Francisco, California

I came here in 1991. My dad was in San Francisco and my mom in Peru with me. He tried to bring me here but he wasn't able to. The second time he succeeded with the paperwork.

It was real hard to adjust because I didn't know the language. It took me three months to be able to say yellow, yesterday, and your. After six months I was able to speak like Tarzan, "me play with ball." Then my stepmom moved here and she helped me a lot with learning the language.

My mom is German and living in Bremen, Germany, with two sons. We fax each other letters at least once or twice a week. My grandma who lives in Germany and loves me very much sends me lots of money sometimes for a gift, for no reason.

My father is a mechanic and my mother in Germany is a translator knowing six languages. I have two sisters living here with me, Gabriella, who is one, and Maria Fernanda, who is three. My stepmom treats me like her real son, never puts me apart from her daughters. At home I speak 60 percent Spanish with my dad. In Lima I went to a German school and spoke only German. Spanish was my second language over there.

> If I don't become a cartoonist then I'll become a lawyer and talk everybody out of their troubles.

Mostly, I miss my family, home, and Lima. We had a beautiful large three-story home there. I miss the sincerity there. There I could talk on the street with a girl my age and nobody would say, "Whew, wow, you like her." There it is freer and more mature. In Peru, people just seem more sincere. When people are walking down the street here they say, "Hi, how are you?" They really don't care how you are. This is a fake automatic statement said to be polite and make conversation. I feel more at home in Lima. I have a big family there and everyone knows me in my neighborhood.

Alexander Collazos concentrates during English class.

They can say whatever they want on the television about terrorism in Peru, but I feel safer there than here. Here if I go outside and if I'm wearing a red shirt or blue shirt, I could be jumped by a gang just because these may be gang colors. Once it almost happened to me and I did what any normal person would do, I ran. One of the big differences between Lima and here is the traffic. In Lima they just don't follow the stop signs and lights. If a cop pulls you over and you pull out some money he'll just let you go.

I think the American government should let in all immigrants who will work. If they are bums or go on welfare and never try to get off government assistance kick them out of the country. If someone calls me a name or says "Go back to your country" I ignore them. I have a strong personality. They can say what they want because I know they have the brain size of a worm and I'm superior to them.

I'm the only Peruvian here at Parkway Heights Middle School. I feel unique because nobody else has the same ethnic heritage here as I do. As soon as I'm out of high school I'm going to college to study to become a cartoonist. I love drawing and making up my own characters and stories.

My advice to a newcomer my age coming to America is don't let anyone talk down to you or put you down because you have an accent. If you think you can do it—do it. Follow your dreams, anything is possible.

Edward Rosa Maldonado

Age 12

Born in Guaynabo, Puerto Rico

Lives in South San Francisco, California

I came here in 1994 to South San Francisco, to get away for a while from all the murders. Every day someone is killed there. If you sell drugs and don't pay the person who is supplying you with the drugs, they will catch and kill you. One of my uncles was killed because he was dealing in drugs and guns.

In Guaynabo everyone spoke Spanish and I had many friends. Here I just have a few friends. The subjects they teach in Puerto Rico are the same we have here, like algebra, but here it is a little harder. Math and social studies are difficult for me. My favorite class is science because we do experiments and study living organisms. When I grow up I want to be either a scientist or the person who designs and builds planes for the U.S. Air Force.

Edward Rosa Maldonado plays with his model airplanes.

On the weekends I like to go to the airplane club and fly planes. I enjoy building a plane out of wood and seeing this object take on a life of its own. I think most humans one time in their life think

SIZE: 9,104 square kilometers (3,515 square miles), smaller than Rhode Island
POPULATION: 3.6 million
CAPITAL: San Juan (population 500,000)
ETHNICITIES: Indian Mestizo, African, Caucasian
RELIGIONS: Roman Catholic
LANGUAGES: Spanish, English
MONETARY UNIT: U. S. dollar
TRADITIONAL FOODS: arroz con pollo (rice and chicken), fried plantains with rice and beans
INTERNATIONALLY KNOWN PUERTO RICANS: Manuel A. Alonso (poet), Eugenion Maria de Hostos (philosopher, lawyer, teacher), Roberto Clemente (Hall of Fame baseball player)
✱ After the Spanish-American War (April 1898–December 1898), Puerto Rico was ceded to the United States. Puerto Rico is a largely self-governing commonwealth of the United States. Citizens of Puerto Rico are also American citizens but do not vote in federal elections and do not pay federal taxes of local earnings. Today nearly three million Puerto Ricans live in the United States.

how it would be to fly under their own power. Some of the planes I design have little motors, others are gliders. With a glider you learn how to maneuver with the wind. The wind can be your friend or foe depending on the direction it is blowing across your wings and how you steer the glider.

First we came here for a vacation. Then my mom and my stepdad got divorced in Puerto Rico. He stayed in Puerto Rico and she returned to South San Francisco. Now she is studying computers and data processing. I'm glad she decided to come here because back home I made airplanes but they just collected dust. Here I can actually fly them. I do however miss my friends and family. But we are going to move back to Puerto Rico this summer. My mom misses her parents and wants to pursue her computer.

The hardest thing for me was the language and getting used to living here. Soon I'll feel comfortable with the language and my neighborhood and I'll be going back to Puerto Rico. I really didn't understand Proposition 187. Like would they want to kick us out of here if we came to take advantage of a better educational system? They think that everyone who speaks Spanish comes from Mexico. Being Puerto Rican gives me the right to come to this country, since my country is a commonwealth of the United States.

It takes time for everything. Sometimes children adapt to a new culture faster than their parents because they are young and eager to learn.

Edward works on his homework.

I love to listen to rock and roll and salsa. I listen to this music when I'm building my model airplanes.

Edward and his mother stand in front of their home.

Sometime parents are lazy or just too tired to learn about this new culture. The parents have economic concerns that usually don't enter into the minds of the kids.

We used to have Indians in Puerto Rico but the Spanish killed them off. Maybe if the Indians had not been killed I'd be speaking an Indian language. Maybe there is a reason for everything, why I speak Spanish and listen to salsa?

This is why racism makes no sense. Every culture whether it be Spanish, Mexican, black, Irish, or German has come from a mixture of other cultures. Where did the original Germans come from, Germany? They probably were a wandering tribe that came from countries farther east. Did they speak German? They spoke a language today I'm sure no German in Germany would understand. What is pure Puerto Rican? There isn't such a being. We are a mixture of African, Spanish, and Tainos, the Indians of our island.

> Don't worry about language, skin color or religion, just stick together.

Gangs, who cares about them. Gangs only separate people, hurt people, but rarely bring the races together.

Pegah Khodayari

Age 13

Born in Augsburg, Germany

Lives in Woodland Hills, California

Pegah Khodayari

After my mom and dad were married, they escaped from Iran, during the Iran-Iraq War, to Germany. My mother was pregnant with me and so I was born in Augsburg. Only my big sister was born in Iran. We lived in Germany for ten years and then we left because we didn't like the country because of these Nazi people. It was becoming dangerous to live in Augsburg if you were an immigrant and it was very expensive. The Nazis began to burn the houses of our Turkish friends in Augsburg and in Munich, so we moved to Antalya, Turkey.

It was pretty cool in Antalya, but it's the kind of city that is more for taking your holidays—not for living. You can't have a real job there because the main industry is tourism. It was difficult for my mother and father to find work, so that is why we came over here.

My father is an electrician and my mother doesn't have a job now. She is taking care of us. I have a big sister who is sixteen and a little sister who is five living all at home. In Germany we had a big house, in Turkey we had a big apartment, and here we have a normal apartment. I liked the house in Germany the best because I had my own room. We had a big kitchen and a garden in which we could do whatever we wanted to without disturbing anyone.

We came here because we have so many friends and some family here. It's nice here.

It would be sad if all the immigrants who come to America are forced to forget their own language because then we will become like an orchestra with only violins in it.

School in Germany was pretty cool, kind of easy. I was learning in German, of course. My first words I ever spoke were in German. I speak Farsi, German, Turkish, and English.

We didn't go back to Iran, even after the war finished, because we didn't like the Khomeini stuff, so we came to America. We still have a lot of family in Iran, but they don't have so much money to leave. Life is harder in Iran than here. They have a very religious regime which says all women have to wear this black dress—a *chador*—and I don't like this. As a woman you can't show who you are, what you are doing, what your personality is, you can't show this in public in Iran. They make the girls do this because without these rules, girls would be too open.

The boy can wear normal clothes, but isn't allowed to laugh at or with a girl. Boys aren't allowed to flirt. This is stupid and makes it harder for girls and boys to meet each other and be close. If the government changes then I could possibly move back when I'm an adult.

I didn't have problems with English because I was learning the language in the Turkish schools. School here is pretty much the same as it is in Germany and Turkey. I've never had problems in school. I only have to understand what is being said and taught to me. I like studying science, math, and history. Some of the kids who bother me say I'm too smart because I come from another country. I shouldn't study so much and I should do their homework. They are just jealous and lazy.

After school I go outside with my friends and my cousin, then do my homework, watch TV, you know, normal stuff. I love to read horror books, romantic and adventure books.

I like listening to hard rock and rap, groups like
Guns'N'Roses, Bon Jovi and soft music like
Whitney Houston and Mariah Carey. I don't like Turkish or
German folk music but some of their pop music I like.

IRAN

OFFICIAL NAME: Islamic Republic of Iran

SIZE: 1,648,000 square kilometers (674,294 square miles), slightly larger than Alaska

POPULATION: 63.5 million

CAPITAL: Tehran (population 6.5 million)

ETHNICITIES: Persians, Azeri, Turks, Kurds, Arabs, Turkomans, Baluchis, Tur, and Qashgai tribes

RELIGIONS: Islam, Christianity (Armenian and Assyrian), Zoroastrianism, Bahai

LANGUAGES: Persian (Farsi), Turkish dialects, Kurdish, Arabic

MONETARY UNIT: rial

TRADITIONAL FOODS: fessendjun (pomegranates, walnuts, chicken and rice), noone sabzi (cheese, onions, radishes, and mint leaves on pita bread)

INTERNATIONALLY KNOWN IRANIANS: Ayatollah Khomeini (head of the first Iranian Islamic Republic established in 1979), Omar Khayyàm (poet)

✳ Modern Iranian history began with the nationalist uprising in 1905, the granting of a limited constitution in 1906, and the discovery of oil in 1908. Iran was known as Persia until 1935.

Pegah climbs on the buses at her school.

I also like going to the movies, seeing horror, comedy, and movies with meanings, like a love story. I hate movies that don't have a happy ending. Even if real life isn't always happy I don't pay for a ticket just so I can watch real life, which oftentimes has unfortunate consequences.

I would tell a girl my age who was coming here as a new immigrant to be ready to learn the language and be ready to make good friends. But use good judgment when choosing friends. If you see they are doing something bad don't do it just because everyone else is participating.

I've seen kids here involved in gangs and drugs but both these activities bore me. I have no interest in wasting the one life I have to live here on this planet.

I think these people here in America and especially here in California talk too much when they say negative things against immigrants. If these people who say these things and visit other countries hear negative words said to them they are going to be upset too.

Here in Los Angeles you often hear people saying, "Spanish people go away, go back to Mexico." But these people saying these statements don't know why these people left, what problems they might have had in their towns. And these people who say one nation one language, that is wrong too. It doesn't matter what music is being played, one violin or thirty violins, it will all sound the same.

Tsigereda Gebre Egziabehar

Age 11

Born in Teklahaimanot, Ethiopia

Lives in San Diego, California

I am from Teklahaimanot, a beautiful town in the Gondar region of Ethiopia.

When I first arrived here it was very difficult because I didn't know any English. I am beginning to learn some English. Probably the best teacher of English is the television because I can be entertained and learn English while watching cartoons.

I have three sisters and a brother. My brother and mother are with me here in San Diego. We came to San Diego because my mother already knew some other Ethiopians who lived here. I miss my grandparents and father. Father stayed because my sisters needed to be taken care of. I hope he comes home soon. My mother felt I would get a better education here than in Ethiopia. My country has had conflict and economic problems for many years now, which hasn't allowed the schools to develop.

I knew some things about America before I arrived from what my mother told me and from what I saw on the television. My mother had been to America before so I believed more in what she told me than what

Tsigereda Egziabehar

I saw on the television. I realize that American movies are made generally to entertain and not educate you, so Arnold Schwarzenegger, Jean Claude Van Damme, and Sylvester Stallone weren't my idols.

My home in Ethiopia was sort of like the school here. We have a lot of open spaces between rooms. It is only one story high. A kind of long veranda.

Around my home it is like a zoo. There is a lot of wildlife and

> I am getting used to American food, though I still don't like food that is prepared months in advance and bought frozen or in a tin from the store.

many trees like a park. Through the windows I would see many kinds of animals, none of them harmful to us, pass through our yard, especially giraffes and lions. Now when I say yard I don't mean this little piece of grass Americans have in front of their homes, but a large open field with trees and water. Near my home we have some beautiful waterfalls but we don't swim there because the animals are nearby. We could disturb them or they might disturb us.

The games we usually played in Ethiopia were ball games, jump rope, and running games. We have many great long-distance runners in Ethiopia, some of the best in the world.

I am Christian and studied many of the Bible stories in Ethiopia, like the story of King Solomon who loved and had children with our Queen Saba.

I have not encountered any problems because I am from a foreign country from my classmates. But I realize that the older one becomes he or she often becomes more narrow-minded when they meet people who look different than they do.

I haven't been here long enough to be able to give an Ethiopian girl my age advice before she comes here. But she will see that in our capital city, Addis Ababa, we too have cars, traffic, noise, and tall buildings just like San Diego.

Tsigereda and her friends clown around on the bus.

ETHIOPIA

OFFICIAL NAME: People's Democratic Republic of Ethiopia
SIZE: 1.2 million square kilometers (472,000 square miles), about the size of Texas, Montana, and South Dakota combined
POPULATION: 53,711,000
CAPITAL: Addis Ababa (population 1.7 million)
ETHNICITIES: Oromo, Amhara, Tigre, Sidama
RELIGIONS: Islam, Ethiopian Orthodox Christianity, indigenous beliefs
LANGUAGES: Amharic, Tigrinya, Oromingaū, Arabic, English
MONETARY UNIT: birr
TRADITIONAL FOODS: doro wot (spicy chicken stew), injera (sourdough flat bread), misirwot (red lentils)
INTERNATIONALLY KNOWN ETHIOPIANS: Abibi Akila (1960 Olympic gold medal winner in the marathon), Aster Aweake (pop singer)
✱ Ethiopia is the oldest independent country in Africa, and one of the oldest in the world. It has remained independent throughout history except for a six-year period (1935–1941). It was also one of the world's first Christian nations, having converted in the fourth century.

Xittali Guerrero

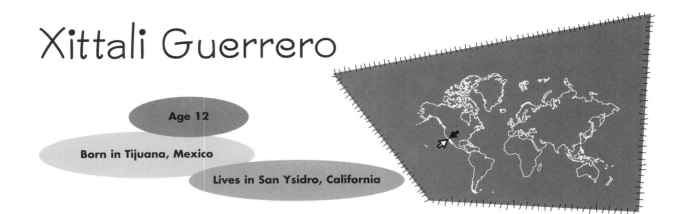

Age 12

Born in Tijuana, Mexico

Lives in San Ysidro, California

I came to San Ysidro in 1991. My mother had gotten married and we started a new life in a new land.

When I went to school in Tijuana I went in the evenings. It was hard to study because there was so much noise from the cars honking and factory whistles. The school was near my grandma's house. I went from 1 P.M. to 5 P.M.

I miss my grandmother a lot so I visit her every weekend. I usually walk across the border and then another two miles. This is one of the nice advantages to living on the border, I can still visit my family and friends without having to pay an expensive airline ticket. Because we are in the border there is a lot of Spanish spoken here in San Ysidro, maybe more Spanish than English. This

Xittali Guerrero takes a walk near the playground

It wasn't hard adjusting to life here in San Ysidro. I heard Spanish in the streets. I smelled Mexican cooking coming from the homes and restaurants.

OFFICIAL NAME:
United Mexican States
SIZE: 1,972,000 square kilometers (761,000 square miles), three times the size of Texas
POPULATION: 93,670,000
CAPITAL: Mexico City (population 8,235,944)
ETHNICITIES: Mestizo (Indian-Spanish), Indian (Zapotec, Mixtec, Olmec and Maya), Caucasian
RELIGIONS: Christianity (Roman Catholic, Protestant)
LANGUAGES: Spanish and several Mesoamerican languages (Nahuatl, Maya, Zapotec, Otomi, Mixtec)
MONETARY UNIT: peso
BECAME INDEPENDENT: September 16, 1810, and declared a republic on December 6, 1822
TRADITIONAL FOODS: tortillas, burritos, mole poblano (spicy sauces)
INTERNATIONALLY KNOWN MEXICANS: Pancho Villa and Emiliano Zapata (Mexican revolutionaries), Diego Rivera and Frieda Kahlo (painters), Manuel Ponce (classical composer)
✱ Mexico is the most populated Spanish-speaking country in the world. Highly advanced Indian civilizations existed before the Spanish conquest, such as the Olmecs, Mayas, Toltecs, and Aztecs.

makes it easy for me to speak mostly Spanish but doesn't help me learn English. I find English a difficult language to learn. I will eventually speak English as well as I speak Spanish. This should help me qualify for a better job because I will be bilingual.

I don't think I will move back to TJ. Here in the U.S. there are more job opportunities. The peso is also so weak now that you can't buy much with it. The dollar is so much stronger, this is one reason why people cross the border all the time illegally. If you can earn some dollars in San Diego, they will go very far in TJ. A lot farther than the peso.

After school I often stay at school and participate in the club Say No to Drugs. We talk about why people get started, gangs, self-esteem, plus we do a few activities, like dancing, hiking, playing soccer, and other stuff.

> I love listening to romantic and rock music. I have cassettes of Martha Sanchez and the group Manna.

My life basically revolves around my family, my mom and two brothers, my school and club activities, reading adventure stories and biographies, visiting my grandma in TJ and going to church there. We often go to TJ to church so we can be with her.

When I'm older I hope to become a doctor because I would like to save lives and help poor people. There are many poor people in TJ because people from the other states in Mexico come to Baja, California. They believe the economy is stronger because Baja borders California. This is why TJ is very crowded. Many people come and see that it isn't so easy to find a job in TJ and realize their best chance of a better life, maybe their only chance, is in San Diego. When you go to sleep in your home in TJ and you are hungry or depressed because you have no job and you see the lights of San Ysidro and San Diego just across the border you begin to think about all of those people, their lives and opportunities. It is only natural for many of these people to envy those on the other side.

Carlos Curiel

Age 14

Born in Tijuana, Mexico

Lives in San Ysidro, California

Life was pretty cool in Tijuana. I was a troublemaker in school there.

Before coming to San Ysidro we moved to Escondido, then we moved back to TJ. We had to go back to TJ because my dad was fixing our papers—our immigration papers. In Escondido my dad worked at a factory making suits. In Escondido we lived in a condominium. It was cool. It was fun.

I have two sisters and two brothers. They are all older than me. My oldest sister is working with my dad in a clothing factory. My mom used to work but now she is a housewife. I still have a lot of family in TJ. I have my uncles, aunts, cousins, and we visit very often—most of the time. It's quite close to get to their home. We go by car or walk sometimes, crossing the border by foot.

When I finish here I'll probably go to Southwestern or Montgomery High School. Maybe after that I'll go to college and study oceanography. Our oceans need protecting before we screw them up like we did to the canyon and forests. Maybe I'll go to the Scripps Institute of Oceanography, here in San Diego.

> I like regular pop music and rap, American stuff. There isn't that much rap in Spanish yet.

There are a lot of gangs here in San Ysidro. Some are pretty cool. But I'm not in a gang. Gang lifestyle is not for me. I play the drums. I'm learning cadence music here at school. You know everything we do as humans we do in a certain cadence, whether rhythmical or unrhythmical.

I go to church sometimes, but most of the time it is boring. My grandmother is religious, but I can't get into that stuff. Maybe when I'm older or if there be some kind of sad event or happening I'll believe more in God.

I think Proposition 187 sucks! What did we do to hurt others? Maybe these white people don't like Mexicans because they see the tagging done on their property and they think that is the Mexicans from

Carlos Curiel

over there. I know some who have tagged, written graffiti on buildings, who aren't Mexican but Anglo, born right here in San Diego. Where do we send those kids back to, Mexico?

There are a lot of people here in San Ysidro, Chula Vista, and Escondido who crossed the border at night illegally. Some get caught, others don't. Most of these people work very hard for little money. If the job was open before the Mexican took it why didn't an Anglo grab the job?

It was easy coming here from Mexico. We are so close to where I was born. I can speak Spanish whenever I want. I speak Spanish at home because my mom doesn't know English, only my dad does. I realize it is important to speak English because it will allow me to have a better career. On the other hand, many Americans are learning Spanish because they see the economic opportunities and benefits from knowing the second most common language in America—Spanish.

Everything here in San Ysidro is okay, I wouldn't change anything. I'm pretty *tranquilo* as we say

Carlos and classmates hang out in front of a mural painted by students

in Spanish, calm about stuff. Why think about stuff I can't change? I'd rather spend my time relaxing with my "homeys."

> It's kind of funny when you think about it, the border is a mark on a paper, on dirt. People a long time ago said this is yours and this is ours.

I would tell a kid my age coming here that they'll probably think you crossed the border illegally —what Mexican comes to America legally? I'd say don't pay attention to what others would say and learn and follow the rules and laws of the U.S. so you don't have any problems with immigration.

Marianne Sawaya

Age 11

Born in Beirut, Lebanon

Lives in San Diego, California

Marianne Sawaya

Lebanon is different from here, it's not really like San Diego. Here we have robbers and lots of stuff like that and in Lebanon it is safer. I don't mean there aren't robbers over there but here you worry about letting your kids go out in the street and play by themselves. In Lebanon we could play outside until midnight and you wouldn't be afraid of being taken or anything.

The streets in Beirut didn't have any stoplights so you could cross the streets whenever you wanted. I don't remember seeing one stop sign so the streets are like a freeway, but the houses are pretty much the same as here.

We had a nice house in Beirut, but sometimes when the war was coming too close to our home we went to another home in the mountains. This place was squishy because it only had one bedroom with two or three beds and a sink somewhere. My cousin stayed with us at this home. But we didn't live in such a house often. Only poor people lived in such houses, but I thought of this mountain home as a vacation.

In Beirut I didn't speak any English, only Arabic and French. Those are the only two languages you speak there. Reading Arabic is difficult for me now.

My mom is trying to keep my French going by speaking to me in

> Here I like watching family and funny programs on TV and going to see cartoon movies like <u>Aladdin</u>. I listen to soft music and Arabic but not country.

French and having me read French books. I'm glad I speak these languages because my friends think it is neat to come from another country and speak in a foreign language.

LEBANON

SIZE: 10,452 square kilometers (4,015 square miles), about half the size of New Jersey
POPULATION: 3,028,000
CAPITAL: Beirut (population 1.5 million)
ETHNICITIES: Arab, Armenian
RELIGIONS: Christianity (Syrian Orthodox, Syrian Catholic, Catholic Chaldeans, Maronite, Greek Orthodox, Greek Catholic, Roman Catholic, Protestant, Armenian Apostolic), Islam (Sunni, Shi'a), Druze
LANGUAGES: Arabic, French, English, Armenian
MONETARY UNIT: Lebanese pound
BECAME INDEPENDENT: November 22, 1943
NATIONAL FOODS: tabouleh, shish-kabob, kbeh (ground meat, potatoes, beans, rice)
INTERNATIONALLY KNOWN LEBANESE: Casey Kasem (radio personality), Ralph Nader (consumer advocate), Jamie Farr (actor), John Sununu (political analyst, former governor of New Hampshire), Kahil Gibran (poet)
✳ Before the Lebanese War in the late 70's and early 80's, Lebanon was the financial and commercial hub of the Middle East. Beirut, the capital, was known as the Paris of the Middle East.

Marianne remembers the destruction that surrounded her in Beirut.

When we left it was nighttime at the end of the war. There were fires in homes on both sides of the street and all the telephone wires had been knocked to the ground. We packed without even planning. We packed quickly and went to this plane. We had one too many pieces of luggage so we tried to put the things in that bag in our other luggage. We ended up leaving some of our good things, clothes, books, dishes, there in Beirut. We first took a boat then a plane to come to San Diego. My grandma lives in Beirut and has since brought some of our things we had to leave behind, to us here in San Diego.

Living in Beirut during the war was scary because you wouldn't know what would happen to you and when the electricity and water would be shut off. War makes you feel uneasy and uncertain, something children shouldn't have to learn and experience.

The war has since stopped but my mom doesn't want to move back because the shooting could start all over again. Then we would have to take a plane back here. It was weird there. It would be quiet, then shooting, war then quiet.

When I go home from school I do my homework and play some games. Here my brother always asks me to play Super Nintendo but over there you wouldn't really have such games. You didn't have mechanical games but regular games like climbing trees, board games, and ball games.

We still eat many of the same foods here as we ate over there. One of my favorites is rice and yogurt, or "*riz-ou-laban*" in Arabic.

I didn't know anything about America before I came here. You really wouldn't meet Americans walking in Beirut and mostly what was on television there was news.

My dad got his diploma in Lebanon but wasn't allowed to use it here so he works at night fixing the shelves and stocking them with Pepsi and

Mountain Dew. My mother works in a building and just does some kind of paperwork.

I have two ideas of what I'd like to be, a lawyer or a doctor, because they make a lot of money and because I like to help people.

I'm getting used to America now since I've been here for four years. The streets have lights so you don't have as many car accidents here. I also like hearing different languages besides French and Arabic. Here I have heard Chinese, Spanish, and some kind of African language. In Lebanon we don't have many people from different countries. Some Americans might not like people from different countries because of their dress, language, and how they look. But I haven't had any such problems.

> Arabs are the people who ride on camels and wear these beautiful robes. I'm not that kind of person. I'm just a regular Lebanese person.

I wish we didn't have so many robberies here. I would like this to change in San Diego. I would also have better doctors in Lebanon. Perhaps they don't care as much because they don't get paid well. My grandfather died because of poor medical care.

I think it is harder for the adults to move to a new land because they are already used to a certain way of life. They have their friends, family and jobs. When they come to a new land it's not easy to find a new home and job. Children adjust quicker to new places because we don't have to worry about putting the food on the table and clothes in the closets.

Marianne enjoys time with her family.

Recommended Reading

The following books provide a diverse view of immigrant experiences in our country, as well as offering insight into what it is like to grow up in other countries, many of which are featured in this book.

Eliach, Yaffa, editor, *We Were Children Just Like You*, Center for Holocaust Studies Documentation and Research, Brooklyn, New York, 1990

Ener, Guner, translator, *Sister Shako and Kolo the Goat: Memories of My Childhood in Turkey* (Yedat Dalokay, author) Lothrop Lee and Shepard Books, New York, 1994

Carlson, Laurie M. and Ventura, Cynthia L., editors, *Where Angels Glide at Dawn: New Stories from Latin America*, Harper Trophy, New York, 1990

Hesse, Karen, *Letters from Rifka*, Henry Holt & Co., New York, 1992

Hamilton, Morse, *Yellow Blue Bus Means I Love You*, Greenwillow Books, New York, 1994

Hirschfelder, Arlene B. and Singer, Beverly R., *Rising Voices: Writings of Young Native Americans*, Charles Scribner's Sons, New York, 1992

Hodge, Merle, *For the Life of Laetitia*, Ariel Fiction/Farrar, Strauss, & Giroux, New York, 1993

Houston, Jeanne Wakatsuki and Houston, James D., *Farewell to Manzanar*, Bantam Pathfinder Edition, New York, 1974

Kingston, Maxine Hong, *The Woman Warrior*, Vintage International, New York, 1989

Minnesota Humanities Commission, *Braided Lives: An Anthology of Multi-Cultural American Writing*, St. Paul, 1991

Mozeson, I.E. and Stavsky, Lois, *Jerusalem Mosaic: Young Voices from the Holy City*, Four Winds Press, New York, 1994

Nhuong, Huyn Kuang, *The Land I Lost: Adventures of a Boy in Vietnam*, Harper and Row, New York, 1982

Rollins, Charlemae Hill, editor, *Christmas Gif' An Anthology of Christmas Poems, Songs & Stories, Written By and About African-Americans*, Morrow Junior Books, New York, 1991

Santiago, Esmerelda, *When I was Puerto Rican*, First Vintage Books Edition, New York, 1994

Strom, Yale, *Uncertain Roads: Searching for the Gypsies*, Four Winds Press, New York, 1994

Thomas, Joyce Carol, editor, *A Gathering of Hours: Stories About Being Young in America*, Harper Keypoint, New York, 1990

Wartski, Maureen, *Candle in the Wind*, Fawcett Juniper, New York, 1995

Wyeth, Sharon Dennis, *The World of Daughter McGuire*, Delacourt Press, New York, 1994

Yep, Laurence, editor, *American Dragons: Twenty-five Asian American Voices*, HarperCollins, New York, 1993

A Note on the Sources

Most of the information provided in the sidebars in this book was gathered from *Countries of the World and their Leaders*, Vols. I and II, edited by Nelia Dunbar and Brian Rajewski (Gale Research, Inc., Detroit, Michigan, 1995); *The Statesman's Yearbook, 1995-96*, 132nd edition, edited by Brian Hunter (St. Martin's Press, New York, 1995); and *Webster's New Geographical Dictionary* (Merriam-Webster, Inc., Springfield, Massachusetts, 1984). In conjunction with these library resources, many embassies, United Nations consulates and cultural attachés were kind enough to update statistics and supply interesting facts about their peoples and cultures.

The statistics on page 6 are from the Immigration and Naturalization Service, Demographic Statistics Branch, Statistics Division: Table 3 (Immigrants Admitted by Region and Selected Country of Birth—Fiscal Years 1984-94), Table 13 (Immigrants Admitted by Selected Country of Birth, Age and Sex—Fiscal Year 1994), Table 17 (Immigrants Admitted by Selected Country of Birth and State of Intended Residence—Fiscal Year 1994), and Table 19 (Immigrants Admitted by Selected Country of Birth and Selected Metropolitan Statistical Area of Intended Residence—Fiscal Year 1994). Statistics include legal immigrants only.

Index

Page numbers in **bold** *indicate references in the "Country Facts" section of each chapter.*